Shorty Bean
and the
Power of the Locket

by

Holly K. Szurpicki

Shorty Bean and the Power of the Locket
Copyright © 2021—Holly K. Szurpicki
ISBN: 978-0-9992323-3-0
Library of Congress Control Number: 2019905453
Szurpicki, H. K., 1976 -

Illustrations by Colleen Szurpicki
Front & Back Cover by Colleen Szurpicki
Art Contributor: NeKeysha Guyton
Text Design: Lisa Simpson, Simpson Productions

Dedication

My highest gratitude to God for all He has done and continues to do for me! What seemed impossible through prayer became possible by faith. The Lord has walked with me every step of the way, He is my shield, my rock and my confidence who gives me hope to pursue my dreams. I would like to thank my beloved husband John for supporting me in prayer, love and strength for every bump and unexpected turn along the way.

My children Jonathon and Colleen for encouraging me.

A special thanks to the most talented illustrators, my daughter Colleen Szurpicki and NeKeysha Guyton. A grateful heart to DaShawn L. Hall who helped me bring the Shorty Bean to life. A BIG thank you to Karen Hardin for helping me edit my literary works.

Table of Contents

Introduction

Back to school can be dreadful for some, but to Shorty Bean it was truly delightful; and having a few breaks throughout the year wasn't bad at all! She adored school and loved learning; so did her best friend and lovable hamdog Smarty. They enjoyed chasing adventure, or maybe adventure chased them? Either way, Grandpa Andy never understood why Shorty's middle name was not "adventure."

Spending time with family can be a blast, especially when your grandparents live in a cottage up north, surrounded by trees and dense forest. There is always a place to discover and daydream. The creatures who lived in the Gazman Forest just beyond the cottage had become like family to her. Each one held a special place in her heart, but change was on the horizon, and it was prophesied long ago.

No one knew the hour in which it would come, but only that it would. Shorty Bean had a golden heart-shaped locket with four chambers inside, and the power would show her the future. White Cloud, the ruler of the forest, abandoned his nest to make way for a warrior. This warrior would change the forest as they knew it and etch a memory deep in the heart of Shorty. Those who lived in the forest, who stayed dormant and sealed in seclusion, would now arise and take their place to begin to prepare for a battle, a battle foretold.

There is a book where the pages are written, and the future foretold

Who lends its ear to beauty, purity and refiners' gold;

A power too great to contain, written upon each chamber of the heart

A love letter, an eternal flame, divinely given and whose Spirit will never depart!

Chapter One

Sneaky Smarty

The teacher informed the class just before the bell rang that there would be an essay due upon returning to class. Teachers can be rather nosy; they always want to know what kind of shenanigans students are up to. School would be closed for winter break for one week this year! Shorty Bean was excited to see her grandparents and spend some one-on-one time with her best friend, Smarty.

Shorty lay on her bed with her hands behind her head. "Only a few more days left of Christmas break until a brand-new year," she mentioned to Smarty. Shorty Bean looked forward to a break; time off from school was a bonus. Although she enjoyed school during the day, she despised the nightly routine of dreaded homework.

They were only staying up north for the weekend this year because Mom and Dad had to work. Shorty didn't like the idea, but she also knew that sometimes that is the way it goes. Dad always made sure that they had time as a family no matter what. This meant the world to Shorty.

She looked forward to some more awesome adventure in the Gazman Forest. It was always hard for her to leave the enchanted place she loved so well. The forest creatures were like family to her, and she also loved spending time with her grandparents. Many wonderful times were spent at her grandparents' cottage up north over the years since she was born. This left her eager to make more memories, plus Smarty's red cape still had space for more patchwork squares to be sewn on.

Grandma Ellie always made sure to fill the empty spaces with remembrances of each adventure they had been on.

The weekend came quick, and soon they were on their way to the cottage. Mom made sure Shorty Bean and Smarty were dressed for colder temperatures. She had two extra pairs of gloves and scarves and hats and snow boots. Smarty hated his mini boots; they covered his paws and when he tried to walk, it looked awkward. Shorty found it quite amusing.

Not long after they arrived, Shorty and Smarty wanted to play in the snow. Grandpa Andy and Grandma Ellie didn't mind; they loved watching their granddaughter play. Plus, the bonus of staying with her grandparents meant hot tea anytime accompanied with buttery biscuits lavishly slathered with sticky, oozy blackberry honey. She had no complaints and neither did Smarty.

The Gazman Forest was just beyond the cottage, and that is where one-of-a kind creatures lived, Shorty Bean and Smarty met over their years of visiting the enchanted place. This year, it appeared as though Thunder Rail Lake was completely frozen; a sheet of thick ice covered the surface. Perhaps she could ice skate, but those who are part of Ben-Jeer's kingdom were hibernating over the harsh winter season. It was fun spending time with her grandparents, but all good things must come to an end, and so did Christmas break. It was time to get back to reality, school and the dreaded nightly homework routine.

Not everyone has a birthday on Christmas day besides baby Jesus, of course, and the infamous Shorty Bean, and come to think of it, a famous illustrator as well. Sharing her birthday with the greats and at one of the most beloved times of the year, made the holidays feel just a bit more special.

Shorty received double gifts not only because of Christmas, but for her birthday as well. Her birthday gifts were always wrapped in Christmas paper. This year she was another year older and wiser according to her Grandpa Andy. Grandpa Andy told Shorty Bean that you must get older to get wiser, and you learn to put others' needs above your own. Apparently, that happens with age.

Shorty loved the sunshine. Feeling the warmness of the sun touch her cheeks brightened her day, but rainy days were her favorite. The smell of dew in the air and the cloudy sky were perfect for snuggles with Smarty and warm brewed tea with blackberry honey.

Shorty could hear the rain drizzling outside and gently beating against roof and beating on the bedroom window. "Aren't you excited for this year?" she asked Smarty as she gazed into his adorable brown eyes. The magnifying lens made his pupils look larger than they normally did. "But of course, I am, because I get to spend it with you, my best friend in the whole wide world!" Smarty said.

That warmed her heart as he jumped up on her lap, and she felt the warmth of his tongue as he licked the side of her cheek.

Shorty Bean was totally grossed out; she didn't like Smarty's salvia on her face. It felt sticky to the touch and sometimes it smelled depending on what he had eaten, so without him noticing she carefully placed her hand on her cheek to wipe off the saliva. Smarty was sensitive and at times before he became offended and thought she was rejecting him. That was something she would never do, so she was very discreet about it.

As Shorty Bean caressed his fur, she reflected. Maybe that is what Grandpa Andy was talking about when he mentioned that it is important sometimes to put others' needs above you own—a great way to live in peace.

The bus arrived a few minutes early in front of the townhouse. Thank goodness Mom was paying attention. With coffee in hand, she yelled upstairs, "Shorty, hurry, grab you backpack or you're going to miss the bus!"

A tired Shorty Bean sat upright. "Oh, no! Hurry, Smarty. Please help me. I still have my math book lying on my dresser. I have a book test today. I can't forget it, Go get it, PLEASE!" she shouted. Smarty leaped up onto the dresser and gently bit the corner of the book. He had more strength in his jaws than in his paws. He mumbled, "What on earth are they teaching you in school? This book weighs more than an elephant!"

Shorty distracted, admired her daisy toe ring by wiggling her toes. The night before she painted them with a base color of white, then added miniature pine trees she freehanded for a creative design. It was the perfect complement to her toe ring!

"What are you doing?" Smarty exclaimed, "Stop daydreaming; you heard Mom. The bus is here!" Smarty used his nose and paws and stuffed the math book in her backpack. He sucked in his stomach and tucked his tail between his legs and dove inside. "Wait a minute!" Shorty shouted, and immediately Smarty thought he was busted. She reached down and picked up a hair tie lying on the carpet. WHOOSH! That was a close one! Once in the clear, he slowly zipped the backpack shut, leaving room for his nose so he could breathe. Mission accomplished, sneaky Smarty.

Shorty Bean hurried out her bedroom door and didn't glance back at him like she normally did each morning. "Bye, Smarty, love you!" she shouted.

"Good-bye, Mom!" she yelled back, but heard nothing from her best friend. Her backpack felt rather heavy, but she didn't pay any attention to it. After all, school books can be quite heavy to carry. She ran to the back of the bus and threw off her backpack; and when she did, she heard a voice, "OUCH!" Oddly she was the first stop on the bus route, and no one was on the bus! She thought for a moment she was hearing things!

The next stop her friend named Napoleon sat down next to her. Napoleon was what some call an introvert, quiet and rather reserved, totally opposite compared to Shorty Bean. He didn't care about what others thought about him. He was confident in who he was as a person, although his dress attire was rather dramatic. He was the only kid in school who wore a tuxedo with a bow tie around his neck to school daily.

Shorty Bean respected his uniqueness because it is important to be yourself. No person is the same; each of us is different. Our differences should not separate us or cause us to change who we are, or at least that's how Grandpa Andy explained it.

Since Napoleon was a little kid, he wore strong prescription glasses. When he talked to you, your face appeared warped. To some this was comical, and to others not so much! Other kids would make fun of him, but he paid it no mind.

Shorty Bean loved his authenticity; she admired others who were the best versions of themselves. The world would be boring if everyone was the same and that goes for pets, too. There was only one hamdog, Smarty. Well, I take that back; there actually is a tribe of hamdogs from a completely different planet, somewhere in outer space. Does that sound a bit far-fetched?

CLUNK! Napoleon meandered onto the bus. He looked exhausted, and by the appearance of his unkempt hair, clearly he was having a "Monday morning" just like Shorty was.

"Good Morning, Napoleon," she kindly expressed. He could not answer her because his cheeks were filled with a slice of breakfast pizza. He preferred hot breakfast sandwiches over cereal any day. As he chomped, he didn't realize that sausage and buttery biscuit fell onto the bus floor.

There were only two students on the bus, and condensation had already begun to form on the windows. Shorty Bean always liked to write something on the window. What would she draw this time? A cat, a bird, a smiley face or maybe even a likeness of Smarty. She used her finger to etch a rainbow and a cloud. At the end, she added a beautiful sun as well. It was a masterpiece!

Her dad had gone to a local jewelry store and took her seashell diamond and had it made into a ring for her little finger. She notices that the sun began to sparkle, and flecks of gold simmered in the clouds. It was enchanting and quickly reminded her of the time she spent with White Cloud when she soared with Smarty down to the depths of the water and found the seashell there.

The bus abruptly came to a halt! It was then that Shorty realized her backpack was missing. She checked underneath the seat and nothing. "Where is my backpack?" she inquired of herself. Meanwhile, Napoleon overheard her talking to herself; and on a side note, she was never good at whispering.

Napoleon peeked his head into the isle, glancing up and down to help his friend. When he noticed a section of the backpack poking out from underneath the second seat, it seemed as though something was inside of it. It was randomly moving. He thought he better check it out, so he got up from his seat and walked to the front of the bus. Smarty saw his feet coming towards him and panicked; he jumped out of the backpack and climbed underneath his tuxedo tail. Napoleon looked like he had a big rear end when he turned to the side. Shorty noticed, but who was she to judge?

"It's up front by the bus driver!" he said.

"How in the world did it get up there? My goodness, the bus driver couldn't be going that fast," she replied.

Shorty went to get her backpack; but before her feet hit the floor, the backpack skipped to her, then hopped straight into her lap. It was as if an animal was in there or something! "Whoa, whoa, take it easy."

Napoleon fell over in shock. Luckily the bus driver had her eyes on the road and not on the rearview mirror. Shorty Bean unzipped her backpack and to her surprise, it was Smarty. "What are you doing in here?" she asked.

"Don't be mad at me. I'm tired of staying home when you go to school. I want to see what it's about. I have never been," he replied. "Smarty, hamdogs are not allowed in school. I could get in trouble, and Dad would give you away if he ever found out." "Look, your dad loves me. He's a ham," he said with a debonair look on his face. "I'll stay in your backpack, and I promise I will be quiet," he said. "Okay, but you promise, no shenanigans, Smarty. I mean it!" Then he whispered in her ear, "While Napoleon is knocked out, can you get the rest of the breakfast pizza that is in his hand? I'm hungry," he begged her.

"Smarty, no. I think you had enough to eat already! You're going to get a gassy stomach, remember? I know you love cheese, but remember you are lactose intolerant. Sometimes the smell coming from your stinky behind makes me want to hurl," she replied in utter disgust while plugging her nose.

Only a few more stops, and then she was at school. There was no telling what this day would bring. One thing was for sure. Sneaky Smarty had better play it safe and not mess up, because that could get her in detention and in trouble with her parents. Shorty preferred to not be grounded in her room.

Shorty plopped in her chair. It was first-hour mathematics, and she had to use her textbook. She opened her desk, but she couldn't find it. "Where did I put my textbook?" she said under her breath. Unfortunately, she could not take an open-book test without it. Then it came to her, "Oh, no!" It was inside her backpack. She was going to have to be careful this time. No one could know of Smarty's whereabouts. The school completely prohibits animals of any kind.

"Good morning, students. Today as promised is your first open-book test of the new year. Please place your name up on the upper right-hand corner of your paper and take out your textbook, placing it on your desk, please," the teacher instructed the students.

A look of sheer panic etched across Shorty Bean's face. What would happen if she opened her backpack, and what if someone happened to see Smarty?

She slowly unzipped her backpack, sliding her hand ever so gently inside. Smarty, of course, licked her hand. After all, he was lonely in there. She gently removed the math book and went to zip the backpack up when she heard Smarty scream, "Ouch! My tail, my fur is caught in the zipper!"

Smarty started to twirl in the backpack almost as if he was being chased by his own furry tail. Shorty Bean tried desperately to hold it still so no one would notice the inner struggle. Thank goodness half the class was still sleepy. After all it was first hour.

The teacher turned around, "Who just screamed? Fess up; someone did it," she said. Of course, not one word—just an awkward stare from the students. Napoleon fell back asleep on his desk and drooled on his desk. Shorty Bean never understood why he stayed up late every night playing video games.

Shorty Bean whispered, "I'm sorry, I didn't mean it. Place your paws over your mouth and be quiet . . . work with me here. I will unzip it."

Whimpering and crying echoed from the backpack. Smarty was being anything but quiet. Shorty needed to do something quickly now before this got any worse. "Excuse me, Mrs. Shandell, may I please use the restroom?" she petitioned.

"Yes, go ahead. The pass is on the wall," she responded. "Take a break, class. We will wait for Shorty to return before we take the test.

As Shorty passed by the teacher, she said, "Shorty, you can leave your backpack in the classroom." Shorty Bean panicked. She thought to herself, "Oh no, Smarty, she'll find out. Oh, please, Mrs. Shandell, just this once?" she inquired. "Okay, but next time the backpack stays in class. Am I clear?" she asked. "Yes, Ma'am, and thank you!"

Shorty took a quick glance of the restroom just to make sure she saw no feet under the stalls. Once in the bathroom stall, Shorty unzipped the backpack and discovered Smarty sulking with his paws crossed. "Are you okay?" she asked him. "Well, a piece of fur is missing from my tail; it looks ridiculous," he replied with a frustrated sigh; and he spun his tail around like a cat for her to see.

"Oh, come on, it can't be that bad!" she said.

"Poor Smarty, I'm sorry you got hurt. Don't feel self-conscious about it; you can barely notice it." Shorty Bean tried to make him feel better, although there was a significant patch of fur missing from his tail.

"What if it never grows back?" he asked. "Smarty, let it go; don't worry about it. It will grow back. I will figure out something when we get home to cover it up. Okay?" she reassured him.

"Okay, you better get back to the classroom," Smarty said. Shorty kissed his head and headed back to the first hour. Just before she opened the door, she cringed.

"Welcome back," the teacher said. Shorty quickly sat down at her desk and took her test. The day went by rather quickly. Soon it was lunchtime. Smarty had fallen asleep for a few hours, but the smells of the lunch and cafeteria brought his ears and nose to attention.

"What is that I smell? Oh, yes, peanut butter and jelly. Please, can I have a bite of it? I would love it," he politely asked.

Shorty Bean placed a few small pieces of her sandwich in the backpack, and Smarty snorted as he gobbled the delectable bites. A few loud burps went unnoticed by students sitting nearby because of all the noise in the cafeteria. Shorty let Smarty have two cartons of milk. She had forgotten about his lactose intolerance. This would be interesting, to say the least.

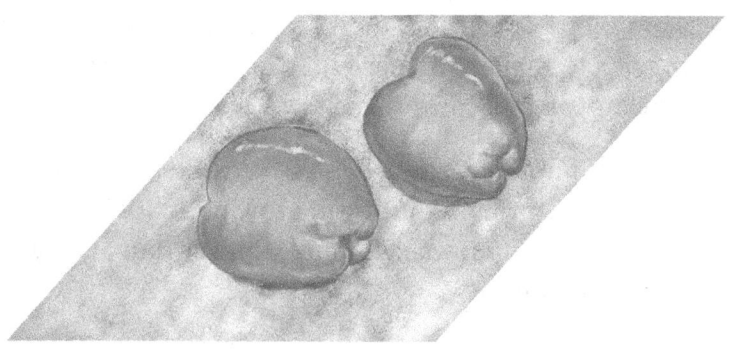

Shorty Bean could not wait for school to be over. For Smarty, being cooped up in a backpack all day was not the most ideal situation, and he desperately needed to take a much-deserved bathroom break. After all, he chugged two small containers of chocolate milk during lunch!

The backpack began to grow, slowly enlarging like a balloon. "BURR . . . RIPP . . .DAH!" the sounds echoed out of the backpack. Classmates sitting nearby snickered, and then something putrid, pungent and rotten began to fill the classroom air.

Everyone covered their noses as the smell seeped from the backpack; the greenish yellow-like mist slithered across the room, heading straight for the teacher. Luckily her back was turned towards the black chalkboard.

Shorty Bean felt completely humiliated, but she didn't let it get her down. Everyone passes gas, she kept telling herself in hopes she would feel better, but it wasn't working.

As Shorty Bean was waiting for her bus to go home, she saw a poster on a pole. Stapled into the pole was a black and white printed piece of paper with a photo of Smarty and a missing label above his head.

"Oh, no, Smarty. Mom and Dad know you're missing. They have posted missing signs all over the place. What are we going to tell them?" What was she going to tell her parents? I mean, if they found out Smarty went to school with her, she would never see the light of day again. "How long can a person be grounded anyway?" she secretly contemplated.

Chapter Two

A New Truck

When she arrived home, Mom was waiting at the front porch to greet her. "Hello, Shorty. How was your day? Did everything go well with your math test?" she questioned.

Shorty Bean nodded her head, and then ran into her mother's arms and gave her a big hug. She was hoping she would not ask her anything else. "Honey, I have some good news and bad news," Mom said. "Smarty is missing, but your dad and I are buying a new truck." For a moment Shorty was thinking about not telling the truth, but she was not good at lying. So, she spilled the beans!

"Mom, Smarty is not missing; he went to school with me." "What?" she replied. "I know before you say anything more, I didn't know he was in my backpack till I was on the bus; he snuck in. I already talked to him about it, so please don't be mad at him," Shorty said.

Smarty poked his head out of the backpack with a pathetic look on his face. He was hoping Mom would feel sorry for him. "What happened to his tail?" curious as she asked.

Smarty glared at Shorty Bean as his ears flattened on each side of his head, then he lipped as his nostrils flared, "I knew it looked horrible!"

"His fur got caught in the zipper," she replied to her mom. "No worries. Come on, Smarty, let's go to the bathroom and fix it up."

As Mom walked away with Smarty in her arms, he helplessly reached his paws out to Shorty Bean. Mom had a habit of overdoing everything. There was no telling what Smarty would look like after a visit with Mom to the medicine cabinet.

Shorty was glad to be home. She put some laundry away and laid down on her bed with her hands crossed behind her head. "How long does it take to put a bandage on a tail? My goodness," she thought to herself. She decided to go downstairs to check on her beloved ham-dog; then something white and wrapped emerged from the bathroom.

"We're all set!" Mom said as she placed Smarty on the ground. "Mom, he looks like a mummy!" she pointed and laughed. "He will be fine; we don't want any infection to set in," she said. Smarty mumbled to Shorty Bean, "Get these bandages off me; I can't breathe." He was struggling because some tape was stuck to his whiskers. Shorty Bean could not understand him very well.

Mom proceeded to tell Shorty Bean how she placed missing person posters all over town, and now she would have to go with her to take them down and Smarty would have to go as well. Mom looked down upon Smarty and said, "You know your folly and because of your shenanigans, you will hit the pavement, and I won't hear another whine about it!" It was final. Once Mom decided something, it was etched in stone. Poor Smarty.

Just before dusk, Mom, Shorty Bean and Smarty walked around the neighborhood and removed the posters. Smarty dragged along looking pathetic. A few people thought he was wearing a costume. They thought he was dressed as a mummy!

Lesson learned: It is important to tell the truth no matter what. Often, we may want to lie instead of telling the truth, which is wrong. Grandpa Andy says, "It's better to tell the truth than to tell a lie." As far as Shorty was concerned, everything panned out just fine!

Smarty seemed to get a second wind just before bed. "Settle down, Smarty; this has been a long day for both of us." He bounced around the room like a bunny rabbit. Shorty Bean removed the bandage from his head, and both his ears popped out. "Thank you, I am itching all over," he exclaimed. "Why didn't you tell me?" she asked.

"How could I? My mouth was taped shut! DUH," he replied.

He always liked hiding in Shorty's furry slippers she kept by the bed. She would slip her feet into them, and then she would scream. Smarty would just laugh. Smarty could make it into the most difficult places like he was a rabbit or something.

Shorty Bean cozied up in bed, snuggling into her blankets and sniffing her pillowcase, which always smelled like fresh laundry. She overheard Mom and Dad talking about visiting the cottage. Shorty Bean felt torn between two worlds. She loved the city life and everything it offered, but she missed her grandparents and the friends she made in the Gazman Forest. That is where she really felt she belonged. Smarty and Shorty Bean huddled close.

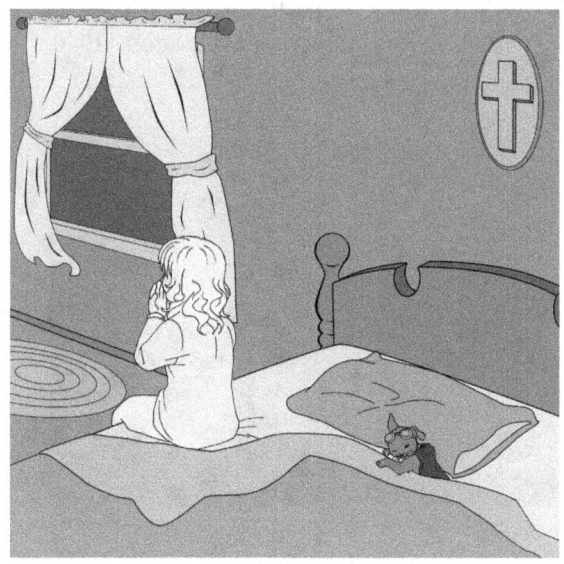

"I am really excited about going up north to the cottage. Are you, Shorty?" he asked.

Shorty Bean replied, "Yes, I am. I really want to see White Cloud, and I miss Mrs. Patty and Tripod and Ms. Nora. I hope that we spend more time with Ben-Jeer the king. Over the winter his kingdom froze over, and the lady slippers were not in bloom.

Shorty Bean now had the locket complete. She saw a lot of things that were beyond her understanding, but one thing was for certain. She was determined to find out what the locket could do.

Mom and Dad bought a new truck this year, and it had a DVD player in it. She could bring animated movies, and Smarty and she could watch them as they were driving out of town. Dad started to pack the car. He was getting irritated with Mom since it seemed like she was bringing the whole house.

Smarty was being very quiet. He did not want to upset Dad, because then he might not be able to go with them to the cottage up north. "Smarty, where are your goggles?" Shorty asked.

Smarty replied, "They are on my head, Silly." Smarty smiled and laughed at her. Shorty Bean had to pack all her precious belongings. It was important that she not forget her lip gloss and nail polishes, which she had every color imaginable. She needed all her hair ties, barrettes and hats, dresses, and, of course, a girl could never forget her daisy toe ring.

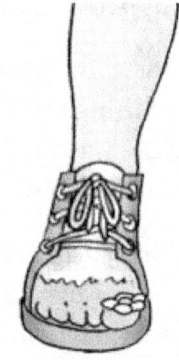

Mom had bought her some new tennis shoes for Christmas last year, and it wasn't long before she cut a hole in the top to display her pretty ring and nail polish. Time seemed to fly by since the new year arrived, and now Shorty Bean and Smarty were only one week away from spring break. It would be nice to get back to the cottage and see the first blooms from Grandpa Andy's gardens.

Dad went to pick up the new truck from the dealership. Mom called it a mid-size van, but Dad said it was a glorified station wagon for which he paid way too much. As he pulled into the driveway, Shorty and Smarty were waiting patiently to see the new ride.

"I hope you enjoy it, because I cannot afford to pay for your college now." he chuckled. "Can I go inside and look around?" she asked "Sure, be my guest." Smarty followed Shorty Bean and just before he was to jump into the backseat, a hand grabbed his tail. "I don't think so, you little rat!" Dad said. Smarty's eyes bulged. "Sorry, Smarty, you must wait outside." A bubble flew over Smarty's head, and he remembered how Norm the wood tick played his antennas like a violin in his moment of sadness. Sigh . . . memories.

Chapter Three

Time Travel

The wind swirled as the birds chirped. Spring had arrived, and tulips began to emerge from the ground. It was a crazy time of year. Mom volunteered at the local food pantry to help those in need and the homeless while she was preparing for a trip up north. Shorty Bean was glad to be a kid. All she had to worry about was her belongings and snacks for Smarty. The car was jam-packed.

The weekend arrived. Shorty Bean awoke from sleeping; it was eight o'clock. She yawned and proceeded to make her bed. Smarty was still snoring as he slept. She pulled on his tail a couple of times, but he wasn't having it. Shorty had breakfast and then picked out an outfit for the trip. Smarty finally awoke and when he saw she had made a bed for him in her backpack by using a small fleece blanket, he was elated! "Well, Smarty, are you ready to hit the road?" she asked him.

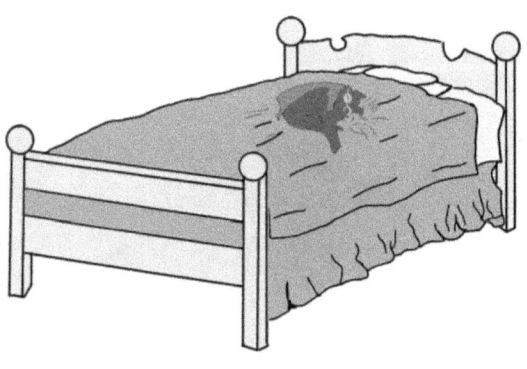

As if skipping around wasn't enough to show his excitement, he replied, "Absolutely. I cannot wait to get back and see everyone." Smarty dove into the backpack; curling his tail he settled in.

Meanwhile downstairs, Mom had a few pieces of luggage resting on the steps of the front porch. "Here are a few more things, Honey," she shouted.

Dad was already loading the car. He began talking to himself, "I went out and bought this vehicle to have more room. We are only going away for a week, and you'd think this family is traveling for two months." He tried to shut the back of the car, but something blocked the sensor.

Shorty Bean with Smarty in the backpack jumped in the backseat. "Well, there is plenty of room back here, Dad," she said.

"Is that right?" he replied. "Well, I can certainly fix that!" Just then, Mom came behind him. "Don't you even think about it, Mister," she said, carrying two more bags. "We have plenty of room, Shorty. Don't you worry about it." Then Dad got "the look"—that look when your mom had enough.

As Mom sat down in the car, she handed Shorty two bottled waters, and she accidentally dropped a bag of apples. A few of them went rolling down the driveway. Smarty watched as the helpless apples drifted away. Shorty Bean was preoccupied, listening to music with her headphones on when Smarty decided to sneak out of the backpack. It was a rescue mission.

He tied his red cape around his neck, tightened his aviation goggles, and said, "This is a job for a hamdog!" Then as if he was being filmed by a camera, he mentioned, "Kids, don't try this at home. I am a trained professional."

Just then, Dad slammed the car door, turned on the radio and began to back up. The doors automatically locked. He put the car in reverse and backed out of the driveway.

Smarty yelped, "Wait for me! Wait for me, please!" with two apples sandwiched in his cheeks. It was the hamster in him. Always packing things away in his cheeks for later retrieval.

He peddled his little paws as fast as he could. The wind caught his fur, and it was as if he was in his own shampoo commercial. Abruptly the truck came to a complete stop, and Smarty ran right into the back. He bonked his head pretty good. What he couldn't see is Dad had stopped at a stoplight. The red glow of the brake lights lit his face. Smarty leaped onto the bumper, pulling himself up to the windshield wiper which was located on the back window. He was sure if he made it that far, maybe he would get Shorty's attention.

Mom was excited about the new truck and began to carefully read over the vehicle's operating manual. There were so many buttons to push, it was like the counsel of a spaceship. It made sense to figure out which one did what. Right underneath the radio there were four buttons. "What's this one?" she said as she pressed it. Dad responded, "That's the back windshield wiper." "Keep your eyes on the road," she said.

Dad responded, "Press the one next to it, and it will squirt out windshield wiper fluid." Smarty watched as Mom's finger pressed the button. It was as if it was in slow motion. Water began spraying him in the face; his paws began to slip from the wiper. It would be a matter of time before he would fall off the vehicle.

Shorty listened to her music, snapping her fingers and moving her arms. "Shorty, do you want to watch a movie?" Dad asked. She couldn't hear him, so Mom helped and tapped her shoulder.

Shorty Bean took her headphones off and said, "What is it?" Dad asked for the second time, "Do you want to watch a movie?" "Sure," she replied

The controls for the DVD player were by her parents. Mom placed her favorite animated movie, Caycee's Cave, An Irish Tale, in the disc player. The animation in the film was spectacular, and the Hollywood cast wasn't that bad either.

As Shorty watched the movie, she noticed a reflection on the television monitor! SMARTY? "No, it couldn't, it wouldn't be Smarty."

Smarty was desperate. He inched his way over to the outside of Shorty's window. As Shorty Bean watched the movie, her elbow accidentally hit the button which caused the window to automatically roll down. Smarty swooped in, soaking wet, and fell dramatically on the seat next to Shorty Bean. Shorty Bean yelled, "What happened?" This startled her dad. He didn't like that when he was driving. He quickly swerved into another lane, and then pulled over when traffic was clear.

Dad said, "You almost got us killed. What was that little rat doing?" he asked

"Dad, don't be mad at him. I'll dry him off. It's fine. Let's get back on the road," Shorty said.

Shorty Bean took off his red cape. It was soaking wet. She wrapped him in a fleece blanket and held him close to her like a newborn baby, trying to warm his body temperature. She whispered to him, "What happened?" He replied, placing his paw on her ear and telling her in hopes Mom or Dad would not hear him. After all, they were not aware Smarty was able to talk. They thought of him as merely a household pet, occasionally singing, whimpering and growling.

"I was chasing apples, and then Dad took off without me. He hates me!" Smarty said. "No, he does not!" "Well, he didn't leave you now, did he?"

"Calm down. You're stressed out. Go on and climb into the backpack; you'll feel safe in there." Smarty did as he was told! It wasn't easy being a hamdog, but he trusted his best friend. She never let him down.

They were not far from the cottage, maybe an hour or so. Shorty stuck her head out the window and smelled the fresh air with just a hint of the Pine trees. Smarty hid in the backpack quivering. He had enough of fresh air for this road trip, that was for sure. Mom nicely asked Shorty to roll up her window. She listened to her mom, and then in a few minutes tried to press the button again. Too late. Dad already pressed the safety lock which meant no one in the backseat was getting any fresh air without parental permission.

Dad pressed the safety lock just to mess with her. That meant those who sat in the backseat would be unable to roll down their window. Shorty Bean became frustrated. She crossed her arms and sighed. Dad smiled as he looked at her from the rearview mirror.

Everyone in the car needed to stretch their legs. They had been driving for a few hours. "Why not stop at Mat and Mouse's party store? I mean, it is the party store 'of all' party stores," Shorty Bean expressed. This place was filled with every trinket imaginable. Dad thought it was a dusting nightmare and most of the items were strictly junk; that is because he didn't like shopping, but Mom did!

Vacation was the one time when Shorty Bean could get anything her heart desired. Mom and Dad always made sure she could get something special. Shorty Bean and Smarty got a grape soda and looked around at all the trinkets.

Shorty Bean saw a little wooden stick with an eagle's head carved on the top and hand painted in watercolors. "Can I get this, Daddy? Please," she begged.

"Yes, you can get it, but that is the only thing I am buying you until you graduate from high school." Dad grinned and gave Shorty a big hug!

"Thank you, Daddy," she jumped in excitement!

Shorty Bean bought Smarty a little piece of watermelon taffy. When they got back in the car, Shorty tucked her eagle stick carefully in the backpack. Smarty was awaiting his treat, and Shorty Bean unwrapped it for him as he snorted in excitement.

Smarty was in taffy heaven. Strings of sticky taffy matted down in his fur and some even stuck onto the roof of his mouth. He was quite a mess, but he was determined to devour every bite of the watermelon taffy.

As they continued down the road, Shorty Bean could not contain her excitement. Visiting her Grandpa Andy and Grandma Ellie was the best! They were an important part of her life, and she was grateful for them and how much they loved her. Plus, there were a few creatures she needed to see and a forest that needed exploring, and she was just the girl to do it!

Each time she visited felt like the first time. Of course, the surroundings were familiar. Grandma Ellie always made sure of that, but there was no telling what mystery lay beyond the cottage. The Gazman Forest was filled with intrigue.

Chapter Four

Red Wagon

When they arrived at Grandpa Andy and Grandma Ellie's cottage, not much had changed. This was comforting to Shorty Bean. It was spring and, of course, Grandma Ellie had begun to plant lavender preparing for the summer and late fall harvest. Once the lavender plants were in bloom, she would clip some and place them in silver vases. The smell of the lavender was comforting to Shorty; however, not so comforting to Smarty. Sniffing lavender up his nose made him sneeze something awful!

The one thing that meant the world to Shorty Bean was her grandparents expression when they saw her. Their faces etched with smiles, and they beamed with joy! This always made her feel loved and welcomed!

As they pulled onto the dirt road, Grandpa Andy was outside on the porch rocking in his chair. "Well, hello, Shorty Bean. Come, give your grandpa a big old bear hug!" He bends down as she leaps into his arms.

"Grandpa, Grandpa, I love you!" Shorty ran to him and wrapped her arms around him very tightly. Grandma Ellie was in the kitchen, and Shorty Bean ran into the kitchen and gave her a big hug.

"Shorty Bean, you look more and more like your mother," Grandma Ellie said as she held her close. Smarty wanted attention, too, so she patted the top of his head. "Grandma, Grandma," she begged as she tugged her apron. "What is it, Honey?" "Can Smarty and I go out to the backyard and play for a bit? He's been in the car for a long time." Smarty stretched his legs and acted like he had lower back pains for added effect. "Sure, go right ahead," she replied with a grin.

Shorty Bean ran out the creaky screen door on the back deck. There was an old crack in the wood beneath the decking and out pooped her dear old friend, Mrs. Patty. "Who is breathing down my door?" she asked. "It's me, Mrs. Patty. Shorty Bean." "Oh, for heaven's sake, give me a hug, sweetie." Shorty Bean knelt and wrapped her arms around her. "My goodness, child, you are getting big." Shorty Bean laid on the grass and crossed her legs, and visited with her for a while.

"How is Jackie, the hawk, doing?" Mrs. Patty said that the bingo crowd was much smaller now that she had flicked all the squirrels. "Have you seen her?" "No, dear, not lately. I am not sure if she lives here anymore. Rumor has it that she was kicked out by mean birds—the black ravens. I've heard their high-pitched sketches before, and they always attack in numbers. "Wow! I hope that is just a rumor," Shorty replied

"There have been a lot of changes in the Gazman Forest since White Cloud abandoned his tree nest not too long ago." "Like what kind of changes?" she asked.

"White Cloud has a son," she retorted. "You don't say, a son? Well, I definitely hope to meet him!" "How does my hat look?" she inquired "You look just marvelous," Shorty Bean said as she winked at Smarty and they both giggled.

Mrs. Patty, although blind, was always concerned about her appearance. "Do you know his son's name?" she asked.

Mrs. Patty tipped her sun hat, "Yes, I do. His name is Little White Crown." She went on to explain that White Cloud was training him as an eaglet in the Gazman Forest. He was to learn many skills there before he could inhabit the nest built by his Father long ago.

As Mrs. Patty told Shorty about Little White Crown, the heart-shaped locket around her neck began to glow. There was power in the locket unlike any other. The power that rested could not be contained nor could it be controlled. It had the power to protect, heal and guide.

"Lunch, lunch," Mom yelled from the cottage.

Shorty Bean stuck her head out from under the deck and said, "I am right here, Mom. There's no need to yell." "What you are doing under the deck?" she asked.

"Just seeing how Mrs. Patty is doing," she replied. "Okay, well, get out from under there and come in here and eat."

"Wait," Smarty said as he pointed his paw over by the shed. There was a shiny new red wagon. He said to Shorty Bean, "You know, we could take that red wagon and go through the Gazman Forest; I would really like to try to search for White Cloud and his son!"

"Wouldn't you, Shorty Bean?" Shorty Bean replied, "Yes, I would, but how are we going to do that with Mom,

Dad, Grandpa and Grandma here? After people eat, they like to take a nap, at least at our house," Smarty snickered. "Okay, Smarty, I see where this is going." "Can I get a high five, Buddy, old pal?" Shorty asked. Smarty took his little paw, and he high-fived Shorty Bean and they laughed and looked at each other with a sneaky look.

They went inside and ate lunch. Sure enough, Grandpa Andy and Grandma Ellie began to yawn. Shorty Bean looked at Smarty, and he lifted his brown aviation goggles and winked at her. Shorty Bean asked if she could go for a little ride on the motor-powered red wagon out back. Grandma Ellie said, "I don't see why not." Grandpa Andy said, "We are all going to lay down for a nap; then when we wake up, you can go on the wagon." Shorty Bean said, "Yea, I cannot wait!" Smarty and Shorty Bean went up to their room.

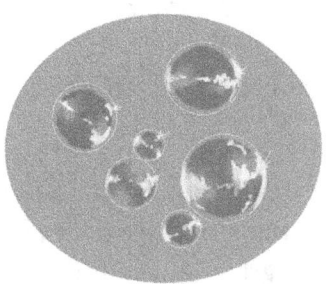

Shorty never liked sleeping during the day, but she gave it an effort. They were restless and couldn't sleep. Mom said, "Shorty, let's go. We need to help Grandpa Andy in the rose garden." "I will be downstairs in a minute, Mom," she replied. The rose garden looked different this time of year; it was common practice to cover the roses, keeping them protected from harsh winter temperatures.

Grandpa Andy restored an old railroad cart with a small motor he nicknamed, "The Red Wagon." Shorty and Smarty climbed aboard, and Mom revved the engine; they were off to the entrance of the garden.

"Grandpa, can Smarty and I go for a ride now?" Shorty asked. He replied, "Sure, take the trails out behind the property and go slow, and remember to stay on the pathway."

Mom asked, "Dad, isn't there an art festival in town this weekend?" "Yes, as a matter of fact there is." Dad placed his hands on his head and said, "No, not again. I just paid the credit card bill. Please don't charge anything!"

Mom smiled and gave him a look. Dad retreated, mumbling under his breath as he walked back to the cottage. Shorty Bean said, "We won't be gone for too long, I promise!"

Long ago, there was a railroad that ran through the property, but it was never used and left with no repairs. Over time grass grew up around it, and it was hard to tell that it was there. The old railroad still left its history behind with every broken rail and uneven ground. There was still a pathway through the woods.

Chapter Five

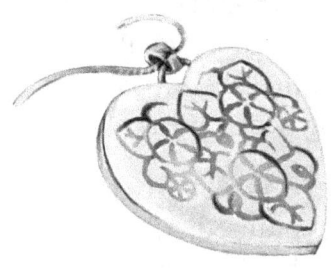

Thunder Rail Lake

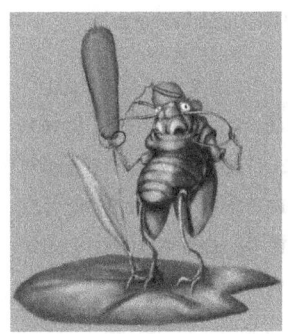

The power of the locket that Shorty Bean held was dear to her heart. The locket was complete with all the golden coins resting in their chambers. It was the faith of Shorty Bean that unleashed the locket's power. Shorty Bean would have to continue in her journey by believing in White Cloud. She had to continue having faith to stay the course of her journey.

She opened the locket, looked at the treasure map and she was to go to Thunder Rail Lake among the lily pads, which is the kingdom of Ben-Jeer, the bullfrog. Since she was there, the lake was completely frozen. The temperatures during winter break were cold.

When Smarty and Shorty arrived, the lake was still frozen. She was confused, After all, it had been a couple of months since she was there. It was spring now, but why winter here? Good thing she came prepared with a hoodie in her backpack. Smarty had thick fur, and with his red cape he was just fine to brave the unexpected cold weather. The temperature change, however, could not stop his goggles from fogging up with condensation. At times it made it difficult to see.

Smarty liked Ben-Jeer, although he was an ugly bull-frog. He had wisdom, and they knew that he could tell them what was going on in the Gazman Forest. When they arrived at Thunder Rail Lake, Ben- Jeer was eating a huge feast laid out on his dining table. He loved big turkey legs and berry waffles.

All the lady slippers slumbered under the water. The lake was crystal clear. With each step she took, they seemed to respond underneath, even the lily pads. As their petals opened, they began to play a sounding of trumpets that said, "Long live the King, long live the King!" It was muffled from underneath, but she knew what they were singing. She was familiar with this the last time she visited the kingdom.

Shorty parked the red wagon by the water's edge, and a French black beetle skated by on two large reeds. He had made a bed of leaves into a canoe. Although it appeared rickety, once inside it was quite sturdy.

"Sis way onto za boat," the black beetle softly spoke. Shorty Bean and Smarty climbed onto the lily pad boat. The beetle took his willow whip and skated down to the lake.

When he came to the water's edge, he gently guided them to an army of lady bugs. They were dressed in soft fur sweaters and red and white capped hats with balls on top of them. Each one held a circle shaped weapon which seemed to be edible. Smarty thought they reminded him of a rainbow lollypop. "Forgive me, I'm drooling," memorized by the lines on the weapons twirling.

A group of lady bugs marched forward and placed Shorty Bean and Smarty in leaf-covered chairs with attached curtains that looked like they were made by spiders. The webs had a distinct pattern as if there was a message of some sort woven within them. The lady bugs carried them on until they reached the tent of King Ben-Jeer.

Smarty bent down on one knee, and Shorty Bean said, "King Ben-Jeer, we have come to petition you to tell us about White Cloud's son." Ben-Jeer said, "You may rise, Yes, I can tell you." He said, "You must first join me at my table for a feast." Smarty said, "Anything you say, your Frogness."

Ben-Jeer hopped with them to a tent feast his servants prepared. Lavish delights filled the wooden tables. Wildflowers, wooden bowls and goblets were set for each guest. However, Smarty's bowls were placed underneath the table. A winter wind raged and blew out the candles. "Why is it so cold here and not at the cottage or any other place in the forest for that matter?" Shorty inquired. "There are some things you just cannot know. When White Cloud does something, we don't question it. He is the ruler of the air," the king replied.

"Come, rest and eat," the king summoned them. The smell in the air of turkey and berry waffles was too strong to resist, and they sat down and ate at his table. For some reason the king could not take his eyes of Smarty. He was feeling insecure about it. After all, Smarty was rather small in stature compared to Ben-Jeer. After the king gave a signal with his wooden stick, it was okay to eat, and Smarty wasted no time diving in and consuming everything in sight till his stomach was bloated.

Smarty had a sneaky suspicion that Ben-Jeer might want to eat him for dinner. What could it be? Could it be the berries hanging off his whiskers? That certainly would be appetizing to a royal frog. Or was it the turkey grease all over his little paws? It might make him slide down his throat a little easier. He could not decide, but he was extremely paranoid.

Ben-Jeer the king did have crazy eyeballs. You could never really tell whether he was looking at you or looking at something else. They never followed any one direction. Then, out of nowhere a large black fly flew onto Smarty's head and became matted in his fur. Ben-Jeer watched as the fly fought to get free, and the buzzing sound caused his nostrils to flare up. Smarty, with a crazed look, his tongue went flying out of his mouth. It was longer than a lizard's tongue. Smarty panicked like a deer caught in the headlights of a car. In slow motion the tongue came barreling towards him like a fruit roll-up, and licked the fly off his fur and it rolled back to him.

Smarty wiped the sweat from his brow. Meanwhile, Ben-Jeer just laughed as he gobbled the rest of his turkey leg.

"I think you thought you were on the menu today?" the king said. Shorty and Smarty laughed it off.

Ben-Jeer said, "Now for the reason you have come, listen carefully." Ben-Jeer the king proceeded to tell Shorty Bean that the Gazman Forest had been taken over by a group of militant otters. Their leader is named General Polio. They were preparing for the warrior to return, prophesied long ago.

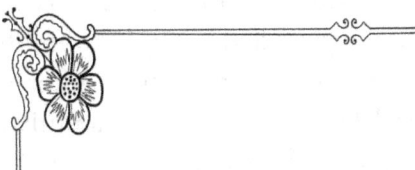

Chapter Six

General Polio

Natural ammunition was plentiful in the Gazman Forest. The forest provided acorns, walnuts, pinecones and various rocks ranging in different shapes and sizes. General Polio preferred to use thistle weeds as his ammunition. Despite his disability, General Polio was determined to lead the otters. He never let his disability hinder his ability.

"He commands thousands of otters," Ben-Jeer expressed. "Can you take us to see them?" Shorty asked. "Yes, it is possible for that to be arranged. However, the only way to reach the forest because of winter is underneath the water. Beneath the ice there is a strong current which will carry you there, but you cannot go alone."

Ben-Jeer went on to explain that a natural spring eroded and merged the Little Dix River with Thunder Rail Lake. Sir Davy is serving under my kingdom for now. Shorty Bean and Smarty's faces immediately lit up! "Sir Davy, the freshwater fish?" "Yes, the freshwater military fish," he chuckled in response.

"We can't go under ice into the water; we will freeze to death!" Shorty Bean exclaimed. "Honestly, I cannot say you won't. Its temperatures are cold, but Sir Davy is fast, and if anyone can get you to see General Polio, it would be him," said Ben-Jeer.

Bubbles surfaced as the ice began to crack in various places. A fish head emerged from the icy water wearing a military beret. "King Ben-Jeer, my fins are at your service," with a gentle bow for the king.

Shorty Bean wrapped her arms around his slimy fish head. Smarty tried to lick his face. "Don't even think about it, you rat!" he warned him with a look of disgust! "Oh, Sir Davy, it's so nice to see you!" she said. "Indeed, it is great to see you, too!"

The otters designed an underground pathway made from tree branches. They enlisted a colony of moles for digging the underground trenches. They weaved sticks like wicker baskets and attached them to both ends of the entrances. This kept any runoff water from the river nearby and prevented unwanted guests from taking up residency. They worked tirelessly day and night to forge the tunnelway and gather food in preparation for the coming of the warrior prophesied long ago!

It had been long foretold that a warrior would come to save all the creatures of the Gazman Forest. White Cloud had left and abandoned his nest. No one knew if or when he would return. However, a few honey furred foxes reported that the stairs were being rebuilt. That meant only one thing: new life was coming to the forest.

Word traveled quickly and before too long, an announcement came from beneath the frozen waters of Thunder Rail Lake, hand delivered by a fish—and not just any fish, a military fish!

Sir Davy unwrapped the scroll using his upper lip and fins. Clearing his throat, he began to announce as all the creatures gathered around the shoreline. Two white wolves with wings bedded down beside him.

It read: "Hear ye, hear ye, on this day, a warrior has been born. Hope has come to us, as the son of White Cloud, Ruler of the Gazman Forest. The firstborn is named Little White Crown. Those of you who wish to welcome him or bring him gifts should follow the frozen ferns at night to reach the nest. They will be lit by the beams of the moonlight." The wolves howled after he spoke.

"We must go then, Smarty." She said, "No, you must go underwater. The black bears are not hibernating this winter, and you both will be in danger." Sir Davy replied, "Very well, then." Shorty was not ready to brave the arctic cold. Smarty placed his goggles on and tightened the straps. Shorty Bean tied her scarf around her head. She took a deep breath and just before she plugged her nose she said, "This is going to be interesting!" Shorty Bean grabbed on to Sir Davy's scales on his back. He was slippery, but she had a good grip.

Sir Davy plummeted into the water, weaving in and out navigating through large aquatic plants. As he swam with the current, he tried to lead them past an old log. It was very large, probably once cut down for lumber and had two large branches sticking out. Smarty's cape caught one of the branches and jolted Shorty Bean. She lost her grip as they separated. Sir Davy was taken by the current in the opposite direction.

She was in trouble. Big trouble! Shorty began to panic and take water into her lungs. She punched the top of the ice above her head in hopes it would break or someone would hear her.

It only took a few seconds and she became weak, the water was frigid, and she was losing energy fast when out of nowhere a light shown round about her. She heard a CRASH, POP! The ice broke open and the current reversed, carrying Shorty Bean to the surface. Relieved, she gasped for air. Large talons grabbed her by her coat, picking her up out of the water and gently tossed her onto dry land.

Shorty Bean lay with her head down in the ferns, utterly exhausted. Faintly, she said, "Smarty, where is Smarty?" No sooner did the words leave her tongue when Smarty was dropped right next to her. Two large wings covered them both, and then a fire appeared to keep them warm. Then the creature vanished. "Are you okay? I was so scared you were dead," Shorty said as she snuggled close, both shivering. "Did you see who rescued us?" she inquired "No, whatever it was came from behind," Smarty replied.

They warmed themselves by the fire. Smarty noticed Sir Davy flopping out of the water. It was apparent he was on his way back. He sang a familiar song, "Triba de la de do, make the forest rain with dew; bring back the spring and shine, for the son of White Cloud is divine. Triba, da, la de da do!"

Heavy rains thundered over the kingdom. The ice on the lake broke apart and sank and the temperature changed, the lady slippers bounced to attention and green lily pads formed a pathway.

The rains would cause the seedlings to drop from the branches of the trees, and then they would naturally make little beds for themselves in the ground where they would live and grow little sprouts and turn into big trees. Shorty Bean knew that she had to get back to the cottage. It was raining, and she was sure Grandpa Andy and her parents would start to look for her and Smarty. Shorty Bean said her good-byes to Ben-Jeer. She could not wait for the beetle to return on the lily pad. Shorty Bean and Smarty dove off into the water, swimming as fast as they could towards the little wagon that was parked near the water's edge.

Smarty was diving in and out of the water like a dolphin. He was doing some acrobatics of his own. Smarty did a paw stand. When Shorty saw his tiny paws and little thighs extending from underneath, she began to belly laugh.

Shorty used her backpack to float her along the water. The current was very strong. Shorty Bean looked back but could not see him. Her heart broke. What if he drowns? She could not imagine her life without him. He was her best friend. "Smarty, Smarty, where are you?", she yelled.

Then he stuck his legs and little paws up in the air. "Seriously, Smarty, you are hilarious!" Then she just laughed. Smarty was caught in an underwater handstand. Shorty Bean laughed so hard her stomach hurt when she saw Smarty come up out of the water with crazy hair and goggles filled with water resembling mini fishbowls.

His cheeks appeared big as grapefruits. Smarty took both paws and pressed his cheeks, and water gushed forth just like a garden hose. They went back on the red wagon through the old trails which hopefully would bring them back to the cottage.

She ran to the deck, and there was Mrs. Patty fixing her hat and swaying her skirt back and forth. She said, "Relax, dear. Everyone is asleep. In fact (as she yawned), I should be getting some rest, too." Mrs. Patty said, "How does my hat look? Did you notice my new shoes? They're green. Do you like them?" Shorty Bean replied, "Yes, I certainly do."

"You look simply marvelous, Mrs. Patty," she said. Shorty Bean and Smarty ran inside the cottage. Smarty's red cape caught on the back screen door, and it tore a tiny bit. Then they heard Mrs. Patty say, "On your way back to the garden tomorrow, could you bring me some more nylons?" Shorty Bean said, "Sure, Mrs. Patty."

Then she ran inside, Smarty was right behind her. They wasted no time; they headed straight upstairs to the bedroom. Shorty jumped onto the mattress, and Smarty dove into her slippers lying near the bed. Now would be a great time to pretend to be sleeping she thought as she heard footsteps.

Grandma Ellie came up the stairs, knelt by the bed and began to pray,

"As night falls and the sky begins to sleep, I pray the Lord your soul to keep. I know that angels will be sitting near by to watch you at night and fly, fly, fly. Tuck yourself in bed, my dear, and dream of candies and elephant ears. Think about what daybreak will bring, when we spend the day together and watch the morning shine and sing. Bless the skies, the oceans, the seasons and the sun.

"Bless Mommies and Daddies and little girls, too, and Smarties and Grandpas and Grandmas, too; and help us to always remember You, You, You. Amen."

Grandma Ellie never missed an opportunity to say a goodnight prayer with Shorty Bean before bed. It was a special time just between them. Grandma Ellie ran her fingers through Shorty's soft and curly hair. Smarty wanted attention too, but he waited. Shorty lovingly hugged her. It felt good to be back to her second home and spending time with her grandmother. It was something she enjoyed.

"I couldn't forget you, Smarty. Come here, boy!" she exclaimed. Smarty was so eager for love, he speedily leaped into her arms. It scared her momentarily. Shorty giggled.

After dinner, Mom and Dad came in to tuck Shorty into bed. "Tomorrow, your mom and I would like to take you and Smarty to the art festival in town." Dad said, "Really?" she exclaimed.

"I can take Smarty?"

"Well . . ." he hesitated. Clearly Dad was thinking maybe he should stay home.

Mom intercepted, "Yes, you can as long as he stays in your backpack!" "Cool! He will," Shorty replied. "Goodnight. I love you both!" Shorty Bean said as she curled up into her blankets and sighed. Smarty hid under the bed until Dad was gone, and then he hopped up near Shorty's pillow and snuggled in for the night.

Chapter Seven

Art Festival

The sunrise was stunning, displaying a golden hue with billowy clouds outlined in the color of pink chiffon. Mom shouted from downstairs, "Shorty, time to get up!" Shorty Bean didn't know what was worse, hearing the dreaded alarm or the sound of her mother's voice. Either way both were irritating in the morning, especially because she was so comfy sand cozy in bed.

Shorty Bean rubbed her eyes. She had a restless sleep, because Smarty kicked her in the face, not once, but three times to be exact. She was a tad bit grumpy with him. In the morning Shorty Bean preferred a few minutes to herself to wake up. Asking her questions or talking right away could set the tone for the day. No one wants to be around a cranky Shorty.

"I bet you had a wonderful night's rest!" she mentioned with a yawn! Smarty replied, "No, actually I did not. I had a nightmare!" "A nightmare, about what?" she asked.

"A woman appeared. She appeared trustworthy, but there was something about her that spoke otherwise. She had long, crooked fingernails and hands and tried to grab the locket around your neck!" "Really?!" she exclaimed, "What happened next?"

"I snarled at her and showed my teeth, like this." Smarty sprung to the edge of the bed; he arched his back like a cat, then his ears slicked back, and he showed his teeth with a low menacing growl. He resembled a ferocious badger.

"Well, that explains why you were so restless and kicked me in the head," she replied. "Come on, tough guy. We better get downstairs and eat breakfast before we have to leave."

Shorty and Smarty went downstairs to the kitchen, and they were just in time. Grandma Ellie prepared quite a feast: bacon, eggs, toast and biscuits and blackberry honey. Smarty could not wait for his share. However, Shorty had to eat first. She inhaled her food; in only a few short minutes her plate was empty. Dad said, "There is no way you could have eaten that quickly, Smarty," he said, as he looked under the table.

Their eyes locked and Smarty threw his cape over the biscuit in hopes to conceal his folly. Then Dad said, "Come on, good buddy, how about a snuggle with Dad?" He reached his hand forward. Smarty was under the impression that Dad didn't like him. After all, he referred to him on one or more occasions as a rat! To a hamdog . . . well, that's plain insulting! Dad was awfully convincing when he wanted something and so was Smarty. So, without hesitation he leaped into his arms, never wanting to miss an opportunity for affection.

Dad looked at him eye to eye and came very close to his lips. Smarty, in his excitement , nervously licked him. It was then Dad noticed something sticky in between his whiskers. Smarty shook his head, "Not me!"

"Not so fast . . . " Dad rebutted. It was just as he suspected. Honey and proof of biscuit eating, "AH HA!" he exclaimed.

Shorty Bean interjected just before things got out of hand. "Don't be mad at him, Dad!" she shouted.

"Calm down, I'll let the little rat go this time," he said.

They loaded in the car and headed into town. It was a short drive from the cottage, only an hour drive away. The art festival was a collection of odd things. There were some painters, artists, musicians, storytellers, jewelry makers, food venders; and one of her favorite fair foods was a corndog with dipping sauces on the side.

"Grandpa, will you buy me a corndog?" she asked "Sure, but we just ate breakfast and you're already hungry again?"

"I am a growing girl!" she said as she grinned at Smarty. It was not a secret that he ate most of her food. Everyone knew what was really going on.

Dad handed Shorty Bean a five-dollar bill as Smarty climbed into her backpack. "Don't talk to strangers and meet us back here in about a half hour!" Mom said sternly. She was all about safety, checking in and reporting. That's just what Moms do, and can you blame them? After all, their children are precious to them; and they don't want anything to happen to the ones they love!

"Okay, Mom, bye." Shorty skipped along the pathway through the vendor tents. As she passed by one, she became curious. The fabric moved like there was a fan inside. This was odd, because all the other tents were stationary. Curious, she entered the tent by moving the fabric over. Inside she saw a woman who was dressed like an Egyptian. She wore beaded jewelry with the colors of purple, gold, silver and turquoise. Her face was painted with henna dye, her hair was black, long in length and in fishbone braids.

There were many candelabras hanging from the rafters of the tent. A glass ball in the center of a table slightly illuminated as smoke rose around it. The Egyptian woman starred into the glass as if she was in a trance, waving her turquoise jeweled fingers around it. "We should leave," Smarty whispered. "Be quiet, I want to see who this woman is," she replied.

Shorty Bean hesitated; she felt an evil presence coming from the woman. Although her face looked as if you could trust her and her smile was inviting, something dark surrounded her. Smarty felt it, too. He kicked in the backpack to alert Shorty. She was a fortune-teller, a woman who through evil sorcery could tell of certain things.

Despite her reservations, she entered the tent. It was then that the atmosphere suddenly changed. The woman's eyes rolled back into her head, and Shorty Bean heard ravens screech in the sky. The heads of two menacing black bears reflected in the crystal ball. "Come closer," said the fortune-teller. Shorty slowly walked towards her, and the hair on Smarty's neck stood to attention. "It's her," he yelled. "She is the one from my dream last night."

"SILENCE!" the fortune-teller shouted. "I know why you have come here. You seek power, just as I do!"

Curious, the woman asked, "Do you know what kind of power rests in the locket you wear around your neck?" She knew about the power prophesied, but she was testing her to see if she knew. Then her face began to change into a black bear with red eyes. The head of the black bear lunged towards her with snarled teeth, reaching for the locket, drawn to its power!

A loud cry came, thundered, shaking the ground; the tent and the candles blew out. It became pitch black; all that could be seen was the eyes of the black bear. "HALT, HALT," echoed through the sky. It was the power of the locket that she was after. The heart-shaped locket radiated with colors of the rainbow and showed a powerful light from Shorty's neck, blinding the black bears. As the locket pulsated around her neck, the evil woman began to relent in her pursuit to obtain the power.

In the very first book, Shorty Bean and the Enchanted Coins, the story is told how Shorty Bean first discovered the treasure box and locket. An evil would try and seek it. but would not prevail. Nothing could stop the power locket and the power of the chambers that rested inside of it. The power is not limited just to the locket. It cannot be controlled; it is the very Spirit of White Cloud himself.

The power contained in the locket was too great for any evil forces to attain. Nothing can stand in the way of White Cloud, the ruler of the Gazman Forest. No power on earth was a match for him! He is above all in the forest!

"Oh no, White Cloud." Immediately Shorty Bean's heart sunk to the pit of her chest; she knew she should not have come into the tent. Smarty tried to warn her with subtle kicks from inside the backpack, but she paid him no mind.

Shorty Bean ran out of the tent, and she saw her mom talking with a jewelry maker. She grabbed her side and wrapped her arms around her. Mom asked, "What's going on?" "An evil woman tried to take the locket from around my neck," she replied.

"I am so sorry, Shorty. Let's get your dad and we will look for this tent and talk to this woman."

Mom immediately went and got her dad and told him what had happened. They were concerned about an evil woman talking to their daughter. They scoured the area, but they could not find her. The tent vanished into thin air, but where?

They questioned other vendors surrounding the park if they had seen any such woman. The response was the same. No one remembered anything about the fortune-telling woman. "Mom, it was right here," she said as she looked over the matted grass and abandoned tent stakes. Mom bent down, "I believe you, Shorty?" but there is nothing we can do about it now. We must move on and enjoy the rest of the day!" Smarty agreed with a couple of licks to Mom's face. Looking over at Dad, he said, "Don't even think about it, you rat!"

Smarty sighed.

"Shorty, you know you are not to be a part of evil," Mom said. "I know, Mom. She called me into the tent, and I knew inside I should not go, but I did anyway." "Next time listen to the still small voice inside and don't go. People who read palms or cards talk with the dead. If you give into their seduction, you will be defiled by them," she explained. "If you want to know about the future, then ask the One who knows it, God Himself." "What do you mean, 'Defiled by them'?" Shorty inquired.

Mom responded, "People who speak to the dead have their wires crossed. They speak to evil spirits and demons which are dark and depraved, outcasts, cursed beings. The reason God does not want us to seek them is because He holds the answers to life. If you are curious about anything, He knows all about it. Why seek death when you can seek life?" "That makes sense," she replied. "I have a lot to learn about life, Mom." "Trust me, we all do!" Mom smiled.

"Come on, let's get going," Mom said. Shorty looked back one more time, and there in the grass was a turquoise bead the evil woman had on her forehead.

Chapter Eight

Fish for Dinner

It was a long day and Shorty was hungry. Dad asked, "Fish for dinner?" Everyone agreed. Grandpa Andy and Grandma Ellie did eat out much, but when they had company, they made sure they made one of Shorty Bean's favorites besides vegetables and salad. Oh, and biscuits and blackberry honey.

One thing Shorty Bean loved about living up north is the quality of the air and the small-town restaurants with some of the best food around. Bert Brownfin owned a small restaurant named "Bert's Famous Fish." He specialized in battered fish and seafood; he also has a huge salad bar with a variety of hearty soups. It was buffet style, and that meant that everyone could eat as much as they wanted. Dad always overate everything, and then he would feel bloated. That's all everyone would hear about on the way back to the cottage from Dad.

Inside the restaurant there was a large fish tank which held the catch of the day. Most of the fish served for dinner were caught in nets locally, meaning they are harvested in the area and a fisherman catches them and sells them directly to Bert.

Smarty drooled at the smell of fresh fish, but then the dreaded sign was found by none other than Dad himself, NO Animals Allowed! "Aw, I am sorry, Smarty," Shorty Bean said with a chagrinned look on her face.

Unfortunately, Smarty would have to go back to the car. "How about I take the little guy?" Grandpa suggested. Grandpa Andy treated him kindly by building him his very own luxury chair with a hook to hang his cape at the cottage.

Grandpa Andy bent down to pick Smarty up! "Boy, you're getting heavy, Smarty. I think Grandma is feeding you way too many biscuits and blackberry honey." Smarty snuggled into his neck, content to be loved, with paws dangling down the front of Grandpa's stomach. He made sure and added some drama for his best friend by showing a pouty face. After all, he had to go to the truck alone, abandoned and now hungry! If Norm the tick was in his fur, I am sure a sad song would have been playing on his leg violin. The life of a hamdog can be quite miserable at times.

The hostess sat them down at a table and handed them menus. Shorty Bean already knew what she wanted to eat, a no-brainer: the fish and chips, please . . . with the salad bar, of course.

The waitress asked, "Would you like to pick out your fish today?" Shorty Bean replied, "Sure." They walked over to the fish tank. Shorty looked at all the fish, and then noticed a fish which looked all too familiar. Her eyes became as big as saucers, "Sir Davy, is that you?" Of course, it was. The hat gave him away. "Help me get out of here!" he exclaimed, gasping for air and spitting bubbles to the surface.

Shorty Bean devised a plan. She'd pick a random fish, and then ask to go to the bathroom. Meanwhile she would grab Sir Davy, undetected; then stuff him in her backpack, go to the bathroom and fill it up with water and hurry to the car so Smarty could watch him. There was no telling if this plan would work, but she was going to try.

"So, which one do you want, darling?" the waitress inquired. "That one there," she pointed to another fish which looked like Sir Davy minus the hat. The waitress used a glove and reached into the water, grabbing the squirming fish. The fish almost slipped out of her hands, but then she tightened her grasp, "Got `em!" she shouted.

Shorty Bean hurried back to the table. "You look white as a ghost. Is everything all right?" Mom inquired. Shorty replied, "Yes, everything is fine. Can I go to the bathroom?" Shorty Bean crossed her fingers. She went to the fish tank and swirled her finger on the top of the

water. The fish scattered away from her finger, except for Sir Davy. She opened her hand, and he rammed into it. She quickly lifted him out of the water, slipping him into her backpack. Then she zipped it.

Sir Davy flipped back and forth in the backpack. She whispered, "Calm down. I will get you in water as soon as I get into the bathroom." He replied, "Hurry, it's hard to breathe."

Shorty entered the restroom, and there was a woman fixing her hair by the mirror while applying lipstick. "Great, now I need a plan B," she whispered to herself.

Sir Davy heard her and asked, "What's plan B?" "I don't know. Okay, just hang tight," she replied. Shorty Bean thought for a moment, and then it came to her. "Okay, follow my lead," she said.

Shorty went into the stall, opened the backpack and Sir Davy shimmied his body and flopped into the toilet water. There was a loud SPLASH and all kinds of noises. The woman standing at the sink was concerned and wondered what was going on, but she decided it's not for her to know and quickly exited the bathroom.

Shorty peeked through the stall and made sure she was gone; the coast was clear. She laid the backpack in the sink and turned both faucets on; however, the water trickled, and the backpack was taking longer to fill than expected. This frustrated her. "Come on, come on!" her hands were shaking. Meanwhile Sir Davy thrashed in the toilet water, "Hurry up and get me out of here."

"I'm trying; give me a minute," she exclaimed. Why did he have to be so loud? His voice echoed across the tiled floor. Shorty Bean's stress level was at it's max! "I'm trying, give me a break!" she yelled as sweat beaded across her forehead.

Then the unexpected happened. The bathroom door swung open, and it was the cleaning lady. She unfolded a yellow wet sign and scooted towards the stall Sir. Davy was in. The backpack was filled to the top with water and now slightly dripping onto the floor. Shorty panicked and made up an excuse to bypass the mop! "Excuse me, I have to go really bad," she said, holding her hands on her stomach as she passed her, walked into the stall and locked the door. The cleaning lady examined the floor and noticed tiny drops of water all the way to the bathroom stall. Luckily for her, she thought she peed her pants. Nice play!

Once in the stall, Sir Davy knew they had limited time. In true "bass style," he leaped out of the toilet, fanning his tail, tipping his hat; he turned his torso in an animated display as he dove into the backpack. What a performance, and now Shorty's shirt was splashed with water.

Shorty flushed the toilet and walked out of the stall. "Thank you. Have a nice day!" she mentioned as she hurried to the parking lot to enlist Smarty for watch patrol.

Smarty was excited. He watched as Shorty approached the car. He was sure she was sneaking him a small snack. Shorty opened the door and placed the backpack on the backseat. "Here, watch this and don't ask! I'll tell you later." She ran back inside the restaurant.

Mom, Dad, Grandpa Andy and Grandma Ellie were glad she returned. "I was about to come and get you!" Mom said. Shorty laughed it off and immediately changed the subject. "See, they say when you go to the bathroom dinner arrives." Dad asked, "Why are your clothes wet?" "There was a problem with the faucet is all!" she replied.

Shorty gobbled her dinner in hopes to make it out to the car quickly. Didn't happen. Mom wanted dessert and that meant another fifteen minute minimum before she could get back to the car.

Meanwhile Smarty and Sir Davy were talking in the car. Smarty took his paws and unzipped the backpack, Sir Davy poked his head out. The car door opened, and Smarty wagged his tail in anticipation to see Shorty Bean, but it was not Shorty. The hair on his back stood to attention like a shark fin, his ears peeled back to the side of his face and he showed his teeth in aggression.

A person dressed head to toe in a black cloak stood at the opening of the door. Smarty could not see the details of the person's face. Sir Davy said, "Show yourself," but to no avail. Then a hand reached for the backpack. Smarty sniffed the air like a blood hound, and the scent he picked up was familiar to him; then he noticed a ring, not just any ring, a turquoise ring, and then he knew exactly who it was.

"Back off, weird rat, don't make this any harder than it has to be," she said. Smarty snarled his teeth at her crooked finger. She tipped the backpack on its side and water poured out and so did Sir Davy. She placed him into a brown sack.

Smarty leaped for her cape and tore it from her. She was exposed. It was the evil woman from the art festival. She grabbed Smarty by the back of his head and threw him into the car. The door slammed, and his cape was caught in the door. The evil woman vanished as she fled into the thick woods.

He freaked out. He pinged from one spot to another. He took both of his paws and swung from the sunglass holder just like a monkey. He swayed from side to side grabbing the handlebars, and then he did the unthinkable. He took his paw and pressed the air-conditioning button and turned it on high; his fur blew all over the place. Next he pressed the eject button on the radio. A CD spun out and he jumped on it, riding it like a surfboard at a wave pool.

He noticed a lever on the driver's seat side. It said this word: Pull. "I must follow directions!" he said, with a sinister look on his face. Then the front hood of the car popped open. "Oh, NO!" he said as he retreated in the backseat in hopes for safety. Dad was going to kill him.

What would he tell Shorty? After all, Shorty Bean enlisted Smarty to watch him, and now he was taken away by the evil fortune-teller. At least he had the backpack; maybe that would be his saving grace.

What Smarty did not see is as the woman fled into the thick woods, she was not alone, White Cloud soared above her, following her every move. He had his retractable gold lens on Sir Davy, his faithful military fish. The evil woman came to a crossroads. A small rickety bridge was before her, and there was no other way to the other side. At first she was hesitant, but continued to cross despite her reservations. Cautiously, she placed her feet one in front of the other. She cringed as she heard the boards creek beneath her feet. Her right foot slipped, and when she grabbed the rail it broke, plummeting her into the water below where she hit her head on a jagged rock and lost the grip on the brown sack where Sir Davy was being held. Her body lay lifeless as the cries of White Cloud filled the air.

Her life flashed before her eyes in vivid visions. She saw herself as a child when she believed in the true light. Back then she had faith and promise, but she opened her hands to sorcery and evil imaginations, and soon she became defiled in her heart. She had turned away from her first love, but He never stopped protecting her and loving her, even though her heart grew cold.

The cries of White Cloud sounded familiar to her; they were comforting. She remembered and for the first time in her life, fear left her heart and she began to feel safe again. The voices inside her head wanted her to curse him, but how could she curse White Cloud whom she loved? With a faint voice, she said, "Help me."

It was then a light shown through the dark forest. From two beams of light, two large white wolves descended from the sky and with them was the son of White Cloud, Little White Crown. He extended his right wing to help her. He asked her, "Do you believe?" She responded, "Yes, I do, and I am sorry for what I have done." When she had given up all hope, He said, "You are forgiven," and like lightning, the darkness etched from her face and she sat up and grabbed his wing. It was then that he carried her to the place of light. White Cloud cried as his wings shadowed the forest.

Sir Davy broke free from the sack and let the current carry him to Thunder Rail Lake.

When the family returned to the car, Dad immediately noticed the scratched seats. "What did you do, Smarty? You've been a bad boy." Smarty put his tail in between his legs in hopes that Dad would have pity on him. "Don't blame him. You didn't trim his nails," Mom replied. Shorty Bean noticed her backpack was flat. "Where did Sir Davy go?" she whispered. "I'll tell you when we get home," he replied. The car ride back to the cottage was quiet.

Shorty Bean ran upstairs to her bedroom to get ready for bed, Smarty followed behind her, but Dad caught him and made him go to his own chair in the living room. He was not happy with him and he knew it. This was the worst night ever! Smarty sighed!

Grandma Ellie knelt by the bed to pray. "As night falls and the sky begins to sleep, I pray the Lord your soul to keep. I know that angels will be sitting nearby, to watch you at night and fly, fly, fly. Snuggle in bed, my dear, and dream of candy canes and elephant ears. Think about what daybreak will bring, as we wake to another day and sing. Bless the skies, the oceans, the seasons and the sun. Bless Mommies and Daddies and little girls, too; and Smarties and Grandpas and Grandmas, too. And help us to always remember You, You, You. Amen."

"Goodnight, Grandma," Shorty Bean smiled ever so pleasantly. "Goodnight, Shorty Bean." "I love you so very much," Grandma smiled.

As soon as the door closed, Smarty raced it up the stairs to the bedroom. Smarty fell fast asleep resting right next to Shorty Bean. Just before Grandma Ellie left, she noticed that Smarty's cape had been torn. She carefully took his cape off him as he pretended to snore . . . Once Grandma Ellie left, the coast was clear. "What happened?" Shorty asked. Smarty explained the story using the night-light to make paw puppets to illustrate the scene. There was only one solution. They would have to go back to the Gazman Forest and seek the help of White Cloud. He was the only one who could save him now with evil afoot!

Chapter Nine

Garden Bench

Morning came early. It was five o'clock. Grandpa Andy relaxed in his chair reading the daily newspaper. The sun soon would rise, and Shorty didn't want to miss it. She threw on her shoes and asked to go out back and sit on the garden bench. This was a quiet place for her, and she enjoyed resting and watching nature.

Meanwhile upstairs, Smarty still had not yet left the bedroom. Frantically he was searching for his cape. He came down the stairs with just fur. He felt naked. He asked, "Shorty, have you seen my cape?" She noticed it was hanging from the chair. Grandpa Andy put down his newspaper and looked at Shorty. "Did Smarty just ask you a question?" he inquired. Shorty Bean quickly retorted, "Oh, Grandpa, you're silly!" That was a close call! After all, no one knew of Smarty's miraculous speech, because most of the time they communicated in sign language.

Shorty noticed the cape hanging on the chair hook Grandpa Andy so skillfully made for him. "We mustn't forget your cape, Smarty," she said. Playing along, Smarty twirled around chasing his tail and barking like a dog. Of course, Grandpa Andy smiled. Shorty Bean thought she was in the clear, or was she?

Just before her feet hit the boards of the back porch, Grandpa yelled, "Don't stay out too long. Rain is coming. You'll get soaking wet." "Okay, Grandpa." They scurried to the garden bench. It was still slightly dark outside, and by the trees Shorty Bean noticed gently lit lights. Her eyes enlarged, and she looked at Smarty. "Firefly jars. Let's go!" The pathway to the Gazman Forest opened; the ferns moved with each step of her foot. Suddenly, the wind picked up and the trees began to blow back and forth. They were home in the forest once again.

Shorty Bean heard thunder rumble, and it became eerily quiet as a dark shadow cast over the thick ferns which lay upon the forest pathway. There came a sound, "Swoosh, Swoosh." An arrow passed by Shorty Bean's face and hit the tree in front of her.

You would think she would be shocked. After all, she was almost killed, but she knew it was her beloved friend, Tripod, the defender of the box turtles. His mechanical leg rotated counterclockwise as he zoomed in on them both. "I see spies in the midst!" he exclaimed.

"Tripod, it's me, Shorty Bean and Smarty," she gently reminded him.

"Let me come down and gather a closer look. Don't move a muscle," he said.

Tripod descended from the tree stump with two summersaults and a one-handed cartwheel. "Do you need some help?" Smarty inquired. Shorty giggled. Unfortunately, it was a failed attempt After all, he was top heavy. He rolled over on his shell. Flapping his legs, he couldn't get up.

Smarty reached out his paw, and then Tripod's eyes dilated as black as night! He pictured Smarty in a green metal military hat with a weapon in his paw. His goggles resembled persuading guns, machine guns, bombs, clearly weapons of mass destruction! "Did you hear that?" Tripod asked. A cluster of dragonflies soared overhead, Tripod believed them to be miniature helicopters. His hearing was sensitive, so anything small seemed very large to him. "Get down on the ground NOW!" Tripod exclaimed as he flipped over on his legs and laid on Smarty. He was squished like a pancake.

Smarty motioned with a weak hand, "Get off of me!" Once the birds dispersed in the sky, Tripod let him go. The army crawled on their elbows through the thick ferns. The seashell diamond on Shorty Bean's hand began to illuminate, and so did the heart-shaped locket around her neck. She lifted her hand up to the sky, and light beamed from her ring. The fireflies' curiosity caused them to follow the beam of light, and they came to rest on her ring as if they were mesmerized by it.

"Tripod, they are dragonflies, you silly turtle." Tripod responded, "You can never be too careful in these parts." Then he turned beet red in embarrassment. Smarty's back itched. Norm was bothering him by moving his antennas to and fro. Smarty didn't realize it was the brown-legged tick, Norm.

Shorty Bean mentioned to Tripod about what happened to Sir Davy, the freshwater fish. He agreed with her that White Cloud was the only solution. He would have the answers. Something stirred in the forest. A new member of the forest arrived. A son was born to White Cloud.

They passed by Thunder Rail Lake, and Shorty noticed a hat on the shore. She took a closer look and realized whose hat it was. It was Sir Davy's hat. Smarty confirmed that it was the same hat he was wearing when he was taken hostage by the evil fortune-teller. "Oh, no, could he be dead?" she said. Tripod replied, "It's possible," but then because of his military training he noticed fin marks in the muddy grass. "No, he is not dead; proof is right there—fin markings." Smarty looked intently at them. Let's go. It won't be long before the sun rises, and a storm is coming.

They ran through the forest following the fern pathway till they came to an open field. They crossed over the high grasses, and then saw White Cloud's nest, grand in stature and new stairs built up around it. The atmosphere changed as if they were transported to a portal. There, two white wolves with wings, guarded both the east side and the west side of the fence.

Shorty Bean removed her shoes, and Smarty left his goggles next to them. They climbed the curved stairs one by one as they heard the screech of black ravens afar off.

Once they reached the top of the nest, a glorious light shown, and the sun in all its magnificence began to slowly rise and penetrate through the wing span of White Cloud. It was as if he was glowing with fire. There in a bassinet was an eaglet, brownish white in color, with golden tones throughout his wings, resting near the breast of his Father.

Shorty Bean was in awe. She couldn't speak. "Well, don't just stand there; come give me a hug." She ran into his chest and embraced him. White Cloud was so happy to see her. Smarty pouted, "What about me?" White Cloud tipped his wing down and scooted him to his side, "Now, now, my fearless friend, there is always enough of my love to go around," White cloud said. And just then an echo was heard. Tripod raised his arrow to Smarty's back! "Norm, is that you?" Smarty questioned. Two antennas shot up to attention. Tripod slowly pulled back to draw. "Yes, it is, little buddy. Who's the crazy turtle?" Norm asked. "No wonder my back was itching. You can be such a pest sometimes," he said. "Stand down, Tripod," White Cloud exclaimed, Tripod bowed on one leg, and said, "Yes, my Lord."

White Cloud spent some time with them, and they told him about Sir Davy. To Shorty Bean's surprise, White Cloud already knew what was going on. It was his divine plan. He allowed the evil fortune-teller to think she was stealing him, but she had placed him in the precise body of water he needed to be in. There is a whole new world where he lives now, and he is exploring new depths of the waters. Most often evil thinks they have the upper hand, but they do not!

Shorty Bean opened her backpack and gave White Cloud Sir Davy's hat she didn't tell anyone she placed in there. "Could you please make sure wherever he is that he gets this back?"

"Absolutely," White Cloud said.

White Cloud had to leave him and told him that he would not be far away, but he must journey and let Little White Crown grow in the forest by himself. He explained that the nest would become advanced and refined with fire in preparation for a coming generation. The foundation of the tree itself would remain intact, but all the unwanted branches would burn away. It was in preparation for a war, a war prophesied long ago. The steps to the nest would have to be reinforced, and forged metal hammered in silver would prepare a fortress for the battle to come.

White Cloud charged his son with great authority for all the forest was given to him. He would rule in justice and majesty until an appointed time. He had a commencement ceremony and anointed him with hyssop oil.

The hyssop was only a symbol of purity for it was divine. White Cloud was the ruler over all the Gazman Forest, and now his son would purify the pending doom that would soon come upon the forest that was prophesied.

At first the news of him leaving made their hearts sad. Little White Crown was not sad, because he knew his secrets, for he possessed a keen "knowing" from his Father. She wondered how long it would be before she would see him again! Spending time with him to her felt like no time at all. Soon her sorrow turned to joy when Little White Crown perked up and began to interact with her and Smarty. Little White Crown was quite humorous. He took his feather and poked him on the shoulder. When Smarty turned around to see who it was, he, of course, hid his feather. Shorty found this quite amusing.

The thunder she heard before she left began to finally produce some rain. This was not a good scenario. Grandpa Andy warned her, and now she would have some explaining to do when she returned to the cottage.

"Oh, no, the garden bench. We need to get back, Grandpa Andy will find out we left." "No worries, I will get you there," White Cloud said.

Smarty and Shorty Bean climbed onto his feathers and held tightly to his back. "Ready . . ." he revved his feet, "Set . . .," he crouched down, "Go!" A "yeehaw" echoed. White Cloud ascended into the sky like a bullet. Norm, the tick, was beside himself. He threw his hairy legs into the air like a cowboy at a rodeo.

In no time at all they were in the backyard of the cottage. White Cloud swooped down and dropped them onto the garden bench.

"Good-bye, White Cloud. See you soon!" she said. Norm echoed and Smarty echoed. They sounded like a trio. "See you soon, Shorty Bean. If you need me, just open the locket." Then he flew off. Shorty Bean looked down at her toe ring. Then she realized two things were missing: her shoes and Smarty's goggles. They had forgotten them at the base of the tree.

"Come on in, Shorty. The rain is here," Grandpa yelled from the back porch. They ran in. "Child, where are your shoes? You'll catch a cold out there," Grandma Ellie said. Shorty Bean responded, "Sorry, Grandma. I'll try to remember next time."

Chapter Ten

Little White Crown

Little White Crown grew in grace and great knowledge, and he was not alone. A great cloud of witnesses watched his every move and recorded it in secret scrolls. White Cloud sent his good Spirit, which instructed him and protected him and led him in the ways of truth. They were one and the same, working with each other, never against each other. That was the secret to their success—unity, not division.

Since his Father left the forest, he was determined to rebuild the nest and put his own personal touch on the place. He hopped along the forest floor and practiced trying to fly, but first he had to strengthen his legs and learn to balance. Most eaglets watch their parents and quickly discover how to do things, but Little White Crown was different. He only did what his Father said.

Other animals in the forest gathered together and built him a place to woodwork. Several beavers brought in wood, while other chipmunks and red tree squirrels gathered certain grasses and small leaves for the rooftop. The birds helped bring everything together. Jackie the hawk supervised the building and helped with finishing touches.

When they were complete, there were a few holes in the roof. Little White Crown smiled; he was proud of what everyone accomplished. After all, he didn't mind a bit; the holes would offer waterspouts so when the rain came, he would have a fresh drink of water. Not too bad! He placed buckets under them, plus they offered some lighting as well.

He hand-made all his own cups and bowls out of sculpted wood bark. He also made himself a wooden bed by using pine trees and cotton tops for additional comfort.

He placed a "C" pattern, acting as a signature, on all his wood workings. He carved seven circular wooden bowls and hammered silver to cover them. He called in seven tree owls, even though they are nocturnal. When they heard the sound of his cry, they came to the top of the nest.

The great owls were silvery white in color and had piercing hazel eyes and a low menacing hoot. Each owl took its place by wrapping their talons on the rim of the hammered bowl. There were seven in all. The small creatures—birds, squirrels and chipmunks—scurried from the nest. After all, the great owls were known to be predatory in nature; and small, rodent-like creatures were a delicacy.

"All of you have gathered here, the Great Owls of the Gazman Forest. This day all will know you as the 'Watchers.' You have been given a seat of high honor," declared Little White Crown. The owls were honored and took their new appointed roles with great respect and dignity. Those who had gathered to watch cheered in jubilee, but it was time for Shorty and Smarty to return to the cottage.

They were only staying for two weeks this time, but when they were together in the forest, it felt like an eternity. The forest was enchanted, and time spent there could not be measured.

Since White Cloud dropped them off at the garden bench, Shorty longed to see him again. It was the midnight hour, and Shorty heard a "PINGING" sound from the bedroom window. She got up and put on her robe and went to the window. As she looked down, she noticed it was Tripod. He had never come to the cottage before, and she wondered what he wanted. She motioned to him to, "Give me one minute." She woke Smarty up. He was sawing logs. "Get up already, Smarty. Tripod is here. We have to go downstairs to see him at once," she said. Smarty was still groggy from sleeping and couldn't put anything together, but Norm helped by rubbing his TV antennas together.

They snuck down the stairs, and everyone was asleep. They had mastered the art of the stairs; Shorty knew which ones made creaking sounds. "I am so glad you came. I have news. The forest is stirring, and armies are preparing for a great battle." He said, "What do we do?" "We must go to see Little White Crown. We must tell him of it!"

Tripod traveled with Shorty Bean and Smarty through the forest to meet Little White Crown. The forest was quite different at night. The stars were brilliant. One reason is because there was no pollution in the country, which often blocks the stars' light. The air was crisp, and the wind gently blew. Fireflies followed them, buzzing and flickering light as they traveled in the deep forest.

They climbed to the top of the nest and knocked on the door. "Come in," he said. Oddly his voice sounded different. When they entered the nest, they were surprised at how much he had grown in stature.

"My Lord," Tripod said as he rotated his mechanical leg. "I bring you news of war in the forest; armies are rising, and they are rising to attack you!" "Thank you, faithful friend, I know all too well, what will take place. You can get up," he replied.

Shorty Bean was saddened by this, "Why would they want to attack you?" she inquired.

Little White Crown explained, "Evil does not like the light, and they want to destroy; it burns them. Those who follow evil pretend to be kind, but inside they rage with hate. Each one of us was born for a specific reason, and I, the son of White Cloud, was born to fight in the war that is to come. It was prophesied long ago, and now this dreaded time is upon us."

It was clear that Little White Crown was aware of the battle that soon would take place, and he was preparing his Father's house and growing himself. He did not fear the appointed time of war; he was a warrior, and he was born for such a time as this. Shorty Bean understood what he meant. Sometimes Grandpa Andy would talk to her about who she was. They had conversations when tending to the vegetable garden behind the cottage.

They stayed with him for a while, and they talked about the forest and about his Father. Shorty Bean loved White Cloud with all her heart, and she could not help but talk about him.

She shared many stories about how she soared on his wings and how he protected her and all about the locket and its power. She found it quite interesting that he appeared to know already about their adventures and the locket. White Cloud said, "If you need me, open the locket," and that is exactly what Shorty Bean did. She opened it.

Thunder crackled and lighting struck in the sky, and Little White Crown swooped down from a star in the night sky. They were so happy to see him. Little White Crown's eyes lit up, and he leaped towards him. His Father gave him a big hug!

"You came," Shorty said as she wrapped her arms around him. "Of course, I did. All you have to do is seek me with all your heart and you will find me," he said as his retractable gold lens retracted and zoomed in.

White Cloud tenderly looked at his son. It was time. What was it time for? White Cloud has returned for a specific purpose. It was time for Little White Crown to learn how to fly.

Chapter Eleven

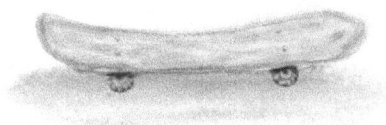

Learning to Fly

As White Cloud spread his wings, his chest expanded and the muscles in his legs bulged. The locket around Shorty's neck pulsated and gently illuminated. A high-pitched screech made way for light sparkled in the night as white timber wolves with wings descended upon them. They had a velvet purple pillow with a gold tassel hanging down from the side.

White Cloud's lens retracted, and a golden beam shot out and covered the pillow. The timber wolves laid it to rest by Little White Crown. The great white owls came, all seven of them, holding a jeweled crown in their talons. They placed it on the velvet pillow, and then perched on the wooden bowls hammered with silver that Little White Crown fashioned for them.

A large pearl was adorned by numerous precious stones like sapphires, amethysts and diamonds. Each stone represented meant something. The pearl symbolized purity, nobility; the sapphire symbolized royalty and divinity; the amethyst symbolized power and authority; and the diamonds were hand cut for sheer spender and devotion to his Father.

Shorty Bean and Smarty were in awe at how the jewels radiated a pure light. They had never seen such clarity and perfection is any stone, not even the seashell diamond she found on the deep ocean floor. The timber wolves retracted their wings and stood on each side of the pillow guarding it, while the great owls turned their heads to watch the top of the nest.

Little White Crown hopped forward to his Father. He knelt before him bowing his beak in humility and obedience. "For this day a son has been given, this day a battle will be won, for on this ground stands my son; hear my words, the warrior has come."

It was still dark and Little White Crown retreated to his wood shop. There he had been working on a wooden skateboard, and he wanted to show his Father his craftsmanship.

Little White Crown raised up his chest and cried loud, with his cries echoing through the forest. White Cloud placed the jeweled crown on his head. Little White Crown wrapped his wings as the timber wolves chanted, "The Warrior has come, The Warrior has come!"

Then White Cloud turned to Smarty, and in his vest was his goggles that he left at the base of the tree. White Cloud bedazzled them with tiny jewels around the rims; he motioned and then called for Smarty to come forward and claim them. Smarty put them on, and he felt like a pop star.

White Cloud stepped towards his son and said, "It is now time to learn how to fly, and take your place promised long ago." "Yes, Father," he responded.

White Cloud raised his wing and the timber wolves soared back up into the clouds away from eyesight. The animals of the forest cleared thick ferns and trees from the area. When they finished, it resembled a small airport runway.

"I like it. Great use of your tools and skill, by the way. I am proud of you, my son; you've done well!" he exclaimed. Little White Crown was pleased that his Father liked the skateboard he created.

"Are you ready to try it out?" Father asked.

White Cloud motioned for the runway to be cleared. He wanted no creatures or debris in the way of his son learning how to fly. Once everything was clear, Little White Crown hopped onto the board. He was a little nervous at first, but the presence of his Father reassured him. Shorty Bean and Smarty sat down on a tree stump to watch him.

"At the count of three . . . One . . . Two . . . THREE . . .!!!!!" Little White Crown used his talons to scrape across the ground building momentum. He felt the air underneath his wings and began to flap them back and forth to simulate flying. But when he reached the end of the runway, he fell over. At first, he felt defeated, but in no time at all White Cloud was there to help him. He swooped him up along with the skateboard and took him back to where he started.

"Now, dust yourself off, and try again," he kindly but firmly said.

Little White Crown made several attempts, and then it happened. He took flight and it freaked him out at first. He was glad he was in the air, but then began to panic thinking about how he would land. White Cloud stood undeterred watching him with his retractable gold lens. He wanted to join him in the sky, but it was not time yet. Little White Crown needed to learn this on his own.

His imagination begins to kick in. He was a jet plane faster than the speed of light. He saw air traffic controls a visual simulation.

Little White Crown became tired. He had been trying to fly all day, and his legs were sore. He closed his eyes and remembered the words of his Father, "I will always be with you." That was all the confidence he needed to land.

He braced himself and navigated through trees until he came to a clear area. Suddenly, the wind changed directions and it threw him for a loop. Oh, no, what was he going to do? How would he make it down on the ground and land safely? He could barely control his wings and the direction he was flying. This was harder than he thought. White Cloud made flying look easy. What had he gotten himself into? It went from bad to worse when he lost all momentum. Little by little he fell. He feared the worst. White Cloud set his retractable gold lens directly on him and swooped into the air. Little White Crown fell into his wings, and he safely carried him to the ground.

Shorty Bean and Smarty yelled, "Hooray! Hooray!" as they clapped their hands. "Thank you, Father. I couldn't have done it without your help," he mentioned in utter exhaustion.

"Trust me, you will get better at it eventually; you will get good at it," White Cloud answered.

White Cloud called upon Tripod, the defender of the box turtles. He gave him this assignment. "I want you to use your inventive spirit and military training and return these to the cottage promptly!" Tripod hesitated. White Cloud set his retractable gold lens towards him and said, "You'll know what to do. Do you trust me?" He responded, "There is no other that I trust, I am your servant. I will do as you ask."

As Tripod traveled back to his hut, the idea came to him in a vision in his mind. He welded a lamp shade with a glass mosaic pattern to fit the top of his head and added a special metal beaded cord on the side.

He unlocked his shell like a door and inside was a traveling laboratory with all sorts of pop-ups and cut-outs, odd inventions. He had a tiny shelf filled with explosives. There was one jar that caught his eye. It was red glass with purple spots, and it swirled like a whirlwind inside. "Ah, yes, this one shall work just fine!" Tripod exclaimed.

It was just as White Cloud told him; he knew what to do. "Up, up and away," was the label on the side. There was also small print which read, "Only take a small amount; may cause high velocity over two hundred miles per hour. Could potentially launch you into space or another unknown dimension. Turtles under the age of twelve should consult a doctor." Tripod, however, completely disregarded the fine print like most tend to do! Tripod was aware that inside was igniting serum.

Tripod took a large swig of the serum and let out a burp so loud and so powerful it almost blew Smarty's cape right off his fur. He pressed a red button, and four metal handles emerged. He told Shorty and Smarty, "Hang on tight. We are about to hit ludicrous speed." Smarty adjusted his goggles and tightened his cape, and Norm the tick lowered his antennas. Shorty Bean held on tightly to Tripod's shell and Smarty did the same!

They catapulted into the sky like a shooting star. They flew so fast they landed on the rooftop of the cottage in just a few seconds. Everyone's hair was slicked back. Shorty Bean and Smarty climbed in through the bedroom window. "That was awesome!" Norm exclaimed!

Tripod helped them in the window. Shorty Bean noticed a light in the hallway. "Oh no, it's my dad," she whispered. "Get in bed, hurry." Tripod panicked. He had no place to go besides the side of the bed.

The bedroom door slowly creaked open. Shorty was right; it was her dad! Tripod hid by the side of the bed and when Dad turned his back to shut the window, he jumped onto the bedside table and froze, stiff as a board. He sat on the bed and rubbed Shorty's hair. She pretended to sleep, and he kicked Smarty off the bed. Smarty was unhappy and shrugged his shoulders and sighed.

Something began to tickle Tripod's nose. It was a leaf that had stuck to his shell. He was trying to blow it away, but to no avail. Dad turned and looked at him. He froze completely still.

"Where on earth did Grandpa Andy get this ugly lamp?" he said as he fumbled with the cord to turn off the light bulb. Dad began to feel around the lamp, "Look at the detail on this lamp. I've never seen such a work of art."

Tripod's shell was quite ticklish as Dad went up and down the base. Then he pinched his nose out of curiosity. "Wow, it feels so real just like squeezing a jelly bean; its squishy. Truly I am fascinated and slightly disturbed," he mentioned. Then he poked him in the eyeball, which was squishy as well it caused his finger to bounce back. Even though his eyes watered, he didn't move Smarty watched in anticipation and he whispered to Norm, "Don't say a thing!"

"Weird, just plain weird." He said, "I bet this thing comes alive at night. Creepy." Just when Tripod thought the torture was over, Dad began to run his fingers up and down his belly. This about caused Tripod to have a heart attack. It took everything he had to remain still and quiet; having military training helped tremendously.

Dad could sniff out anything. Shorty Bean knew if she didn't try and distract him, he may figure out the lamp on the bedside table was in fact a real turtle. Tripod's eyes bulged and Shorty wasted no time.

"Dad, will you give me one last hug before bed?" she asked

"Absolutely!" he replied as Shorty Bean threw herself into his arms. Then he left the room and went back downstairs to bed. "Tripod, the coast is clear; you are so lucky, Dad didn't figure out it was you."

Then Tripod jumped down from the bedside table; he opened his shell and grabbed some more serum. He felt hydrated; he needed a drink. "I have never felt so violated in all my life. Do you know how hard it was not to laugh, cry or even sneeze?" he exclaimed. Shorty Bean felt sorry for him, but also thought is was quite humorous.

Tripod pulled the chain and the green light bulb. "Good-bye for now. I have to get out of here and put this behind me," he said as he bolted into the sky like a rocket. Shorty Bean and Smarty watched him from the window, and all they could see were lights randomly jumping in and out of the stars.

The next morning, Grandpa Andy and Grandma Ellie, Mom and Dad sat on the front porch reminiscing. There were black bear sightings in the area. Grandpa Andy was really upset; there was a local beaver that settled in on his property. The beaver was always up to no good.

Grandpa mentioned he was sitting in his favorite chair, reading the newspaper and suddenly a tree fell over right next to him while he was looking out the window.

He heard this evil laugh. "AH HA HA, HEEE HEE HEE." Then whatever it was ran off into the woods. Grandpa Andy lived up north most of his life; he learned animal prints. He discovered that it was a beaver. Where did he come from? Most beavers remain near a body of water, and there was a lake down the road from the cottage.

After close examination he discovered it was a beaver and not a small one either; he was large, the size of a black bear cub. This made Smarty quiver, After all, he was terrified of the black bears and didn't want anything to do with them. He knew Grandpa Andy favored him, so he took the opportunity to fall apart emotionally in his arms. Dad rolled his eyes and said, "You rat!" "Hey, Hey, now that's enough of that; he's just a whittle guy," Grandpa Andy replied in a baby's voice.

Shorty asked her Mom, "Do you think we can stay a few more days?" "Sure, we were planning on staying till Easter."

It looked like they were staying till Easter, and that was a fun time. Grandma Ellie made a feast not to be believed—honey-baked ham; deviled eggs; creamy macaroni and cheese, the cheesiest on the planet; fresh pies; cakes and cookies; and an Easter egg hunt. Eggs filled with money, chocolate, all sorts of candies and fake plastic grass which Norm the tick particularly liked.

Shorty had to control Smarty's candy intake during this season, well, actually in any season. Chocolate made him have horrible gas, and it was hard to sleep next to him with garbage smells seeping out of his red cape. Smarty had no self-control when it came to sugar, but blackberry honey was his favorite sweet snack.

Chapter Twelve

A Vision Remembered

S horty Bean asked Grandpa, "When we are finished eating, can I go out back to the rose garden for a bit?"

"Sure, I would love to join you, but I'll need to help Grandma clean up the kitchen first, perhaps after," he replied.

"Okay, you bet! Come out when you want to, Grandpa."

"I'll make sure of that," he replied.

Shorty Bean and Smarty went behind the cottage and walked to the rose garden. She glanced around the property and noticed trees randomly moving. "What was going on?" she thought to herself. She heard a SWOOSH-ING sound and then KAPOOSH! A huge tree fell over across the yard and she saw a shadow; something scurried back into the thick ferns. Perhaps it was that large pesky beaver Grandpa Andy couldn't stand, a true beaver nemesis. Unexpectedly, another tree dropped. This one was close to her. The backdoor at the cottage slammed, and out came Grandpa Andy armed with a weapon in his hand and a surly look etched on his face.

"YOU RACSAL, YOU VARMINT, I warned you! Now you're going to get it!" he yelled as he charged the beaver with an air soft gun. Shorty Bean was amazed that he could run that fast; he was older and meandered about. She never knew he was that fast. Although Grandpa Andy did not like the beaver, he had no intention of killing him. He just wanted to stir him up a bit and get him off his property.

The beaver evilly laughed as he fled back into the heavy ferns to avoid Grandpa Andy. Grandpa tried to keep up with the beaver, but to no avail. Soon he was out of breath, and the ferns were thick; the beaver had vanished from their sight. Grandpa Andy walked back to the cottage defeated. When Shorty Bean saw him in the field, she said, "It's okay, Grandpa. You will get him some day." "I know I will," he replied.

All of them went inside for dinner. Grandma Ellie made tacos with all the fixings. A favorite meal for Shorty Bean since she loved greens and diced vegetables.

As they sat down for dinner, Shorty Bean held the locket around her neck tightly. She wanted to get back to the forest and see Little White Crown. Also, she still could not forget about the war that was coming and the news Tripod told them about. She missed Ms. Nora, the Irish porcupine. She always had a way of cheering her up, and she wanted to see her. It had been a while since they visited with each other.

"Dig in, everyone," Grandma Ellie said. "Shouldn't we say a prayer of thanksgiving?" Shorty asked. "Yes, go ahead, Dear," Grandma replied.

Shorty closed her eyes and said, "Thank you, God, for all our food and thank you for Grandpa Andy and Grandma Ellie and Smarty and Mom and Dad, too. Amen."

"That was a beautiful prayer," Grandpa Andy mentioned.

Shorty Bean watched as Smarty paraded around the kitchen table wearing a sombrero multi-colored hat. He snapped his paws and flipped his cape. She could see through the hair on Smarty's back. It appeared as though Norm the tick was riding Smarty like a bull. Faintly, she heard, "Andale, Andale," meaning, "Let's go, let's go!"

Everyone laughed at him. He soaked up the attention in true hamdog fashion.

Meanwhile in the forest, an army of otters were gaining strength, building forts and underground pathways preparing for the war which was to come. They were preparing for the battle that had been prophesied long ago. General Polio was a large otter with a handlebar mustache, and a mohawk on the top of his head. He also used two metal braces he operated from each side of his body. He supervised the otters working hard to prepare for war.

After dinner, Shorty Bean and Smarty wanted to go to the rose garden, so they walked hand in hand out to the back of the cottage. Grandpa Andy said, "I will be out in a little bit. Watch out for the pesky beaver."

Shorty Bean said, "All right, Grandpa. I will." Once Smarty and Shorty were outside, they wasted no time. As they passed by the purple amethyst rose down the pathway from the rose garden, a soft wind came blowing through her hair; the locket opened, and a map of the forest appeared.

Then she said," Shorty Bean, you must travel and see Ms. Nora." Then her petals left and flew into the wind. Shorty Bean followed the white fence and headed to Nussle Ridge Creek to the home of Ms. Nora, the Irish porcupine.

When they arrived, they knocked on her door and Ms Nora said, "Good day to ya, Shorty Bean, and to your faithful companion, Smarty." "Ms. Nora, I have missed you so much!" Shorty exclaimed

"Welcome, welcome," she said. "Come in and sit down with me, child. I must tell you some news," Ms. Nora said. Shorty Bean was excited to hear what Ms. Nora had to tell her.

"Shorty Bean you must travel and see Ms. Nora." Ms. Nora placed a brick of peat moss in the fire, and the gold coin of fire illuminated on her mantle just above the fireplace. She sat down in her wicker wooden chair.

"The forest is stirring; the war is upon us, my dear. It's not the same in the forest. It has become dark, and I find myself trusting less and less of the creatures."

"Yes, Tripod spoke of this war," she replied.

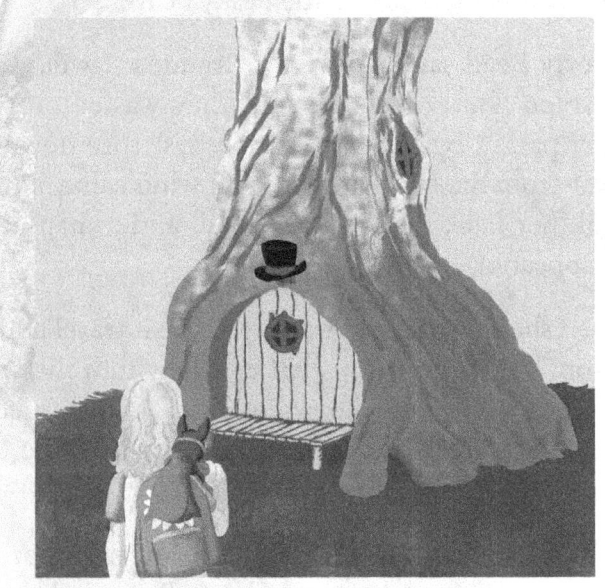

"Yes, my dear, it certainly is, and you have seen it, remember?" she replied. Shorty Bean stared intently into the fire, and then she remembered the vision. She had discovered the coin of fire that the earth was darkened, and she was carried off by two white timber wolves to the place of light. There she stood before White Cloud and the place of judgment; a vision flashed before her. It was the white owls that held the scroll of names that were written upon it. Those that were not written in this scroll would be sent down to the lake of lava in the depths of the earth.

"I remember, yes, I do," Shorty said.

Ms. Nora noticed Shorty Bean involved in deep thought and told her to listen carefully. "You see, the coin has an Irish fable man say, for a man died that day." "What do you mean?" Shorty Bean asked. "Who died, Ms. Nora?"

"The Great One, my dear. Long ago there was a special place in the land where a man was known as the son of the light. Shorty Bean had heard this before, and she was beginning to understand it now more than ever. "Is this son of light, Little White Crown?" she asked her. "Yes, it is," she replied

"Oh no, he mentioned he was going to battle, but he never said he would die!" Shorty Bean put her hands over her eyes and began to weep.

"Listen to the rest of the riddle, my dear . . . A man of which no darkness was in sight, a man who shined as bright as the light, which saved us all from doom and gloom and gave us life. He died and rose again, you see, to save the world and pardon me. Light, bright, yes, yes, this man of light." Ms. Nora danced a gig and laughed with glee.

Norm the tick emerged from Smarty's cape and said, "An uproar between good and evil exposed in the universe. Good found a dwelling place in the heights of the universe, while those who practiced evil were hurled down to the earth. Evil hated the good for one reason, because when the deeds of darkness are exposed to the light, they are no longer hidden. Evil likes to hide its true intentions by using an outward façade, but inward is corruption, evil intention and manipulation. White Cloud ruled the forest and to stop the evil from covering the ground, he devised a plan. He sent a warrior, his very own son, to claim ownership of the land and all the creatures that possess it. At least that is what my Father told me before he died."

"Where did you come from?" Smarty inquired. Most often Norm was ticking him off, but he never realized ticks could be that knowledgeable. It was clear Norm was not the average brown-legged tick.

There were many questions running through Shorty's mind, and not all of them would be answered, she knew that. One thing was certain, she needed to warn Little White Crown of his pending doom.

Ms. Nora read her mind, "Child, you cannot change the prophecy. He must die, but he won't die forever. He is not like you and me. He is everlasting." "Really?" "Yes, come, sip your tea and dance with me." Shorty Bean perked up and danced with Ms. Nora. She swept the floor with her broom. Smarty took advantage of the abandoned teacup licking it clean.

Chapter Thirteen

Long Ago

The vision remembered by Shorty brought fond memories. The riddle she once heard Ms. Nora mention said, "This man of light." Shorty had a suspicion that the man of light she was referring to was Little White Crown.

One thing that Grandpa Andy loved about Shorty is she always asked questions. She let her mind remain in a constant state of curiosity and creativity. After all, how can you learn if you don't ask questions? Without hesitation, "Ms. Nora, when you said this man of light, did you mean Little White Crown? Is that the man?" she inquired.

"Yes, my dear, it is him. He is this man of light, which no darkness was in sight." She knew it, her suspicion was right on! Ms. Nora gently ran her claws through her hair, "My child, never let go of your faith, hold on tight and remember the light will shine even in the night, bright, bright!" "Thank you, Ms. Nora. You always make me smile," Shorty said.

"Bright light," she sang and then began to dance a gig while sweeping with her wicker broom. The time came for Shorty, Smarty and Norm to leave Ms. Nora's tree-house. Smarty climbed in her backpack, and they waved good-bye as they headed back down the pathway of the dense ferns to reach the rose garden.

As she arrived, Grandpa Andy was patiently waiting for her. It was like she had never left. "I came to spend some time with you guys. Where have you been?" Grandpa Andy questioned. "Oh, you know, just here and there, exploring and adventuring . . ." Shorty responded with eyes wide open!

It appeared Shorty Bean and Smarty yet again were in the clear, or were they? They sat down and talked for a while and reminisced about the times they had shared and how special this time was that she and her family had come to visit them at their cottage.

Smarty adored Grandpa Andy. Smarty curled in his lap and stared into his glasses. He liked how he looked in the reflection of the lens. Grandpa gently stroked his head. Love is powerful, and loving someone for who they are is what love truly is. Even though Dad gave Smarty a hard time, Grandpa Andy, on the other hand, spoiled him by always giving him attention and, of course, designing and building his very own chair at the cottage which he took full advantage of as a privileged hamdog.

Grandpa Andy knew Shorty well and noticed she looked rather sad. He asked her, "What is the matter, darling?" "Grandpa, why do people have to die?" she asked. "Well, that is a great question. I have often wondered about that myself. There are many reasons people die. For instance, soldiers die defending freedom; sometimes the innocent die because of hatred by others; still people die because it is their appointed time. We never know when someone will die. What we do know is that although the physical body may die, we are more than just a physical body. We have a soul and that soul lives on." "So, are you saying we never die?" Shorty asked. "Our soul never dies, only our body. Does that make sense?" Grandpa asked.

"Yes, I think I understand," Shorty nodded. "I knew you would, my smart girl!" Grandpa grinned.

A shadow passed by them; the hairs on Grandpa Andy's neck stood to attention. What on earth was it? He didn't alert Shorty Bean, he didn't want to scare her, but he knew something was not right.

Shorty, Smarty laid down in the grass. Norm crawled out from Smarty's fur. He felt safe in the grass. He meandered around stretching his multiple legs. Grandpa Andy became suddenly tired. All the fresh air made him want to take an afternoon snooze. "I'm going in to take a nap," he said. "Are the two of you going to hang out here for a while?"

"Yes, we are, we are going to watch the clouds," Shorty sighed.

"My Little Dreamer," Grandpa said. "Have a good time, and keep a close eye out for the beaver. He is sneaky. I don't want either of you to get hurt." "We will. Have a nice nap, Grandpa!" she said.

Shorty and Smarty watched the clouds, and as they formed, shapes appeared. Smarty saw a candy cane and a scruffy dog, and Shorty noticed an ice cream cone and a rather large humpback whale.

Without warning the clouds became thick, a powerful wind formed and the locket around Shorty Bean's neck began to illuminate, pulsating like the beat of a heart. It was time to get back to the forest and see Little White Crown, but where was he and how could she get there? There was only one way to find out. The locket would show her. She saw on the map an unusually large tree. That is where they needed to go. "Come on, Smarty. It's time to go on an adventure," she loudly exclaimed.

They began their journey walking down the dense fern pathway when they heard a voice thunder as it spoke, with great authority and it sounded familiar. Where had they heard this before? Who could it be? At first Shorty Bean thought maybe it was White Cloud. The voice was similar, but she knew it was someone else.

As they came closer, there was a large opening through the forest. Soon they realized that they were not alone. There were numerous creatures in the sky and all over the ground. Animals were perched on tree branches and large boulders.

A vast army of otters surrounded the camp, and one distinct otter stood out from the rest; it was General Polio. She had never seen so many creatures of the forest; there were otters, beavers, fishes, lions, tigers, bears, wolverines, cougars, foxes, rabbits, rodents, insects and countless birds of the air. Smarty kept his goggles on tight and his cape snug; he stayed in the backpack for added protection and security.

Little White Crown was perched high on a tree. He said, "You have heard and have been preparing for war, a battle between good and evil, and this is true. Choose today which side you want to be on, evil or good. If you choose good, you choose me and not a hair on your head will be harmed. Come to my right side. I will mark you by placing a seal upon your head."

After he had finished speaking, a mean looking wolverine stepped forward and he had a smirk on his face with a devilish look in his eye. "It is Jade your majesty. At your service, Little White Crown," he smirked, showing his gnarly yellowish green teeth. It was clear he did not want good; he was evil and was hoping to trick Little White Crown, but he was no fool and he knew exactly what he was trying to do. "Why do you seek my army, Jade?" he asked. "I am a humble servant and want to serve a king, a righteous king." He sneered pacing back and forth. Little White Crown raised his left wing and pointed it to the left. Two white wolves with wings ushered him on the other side. Jade the evil wolverine did not like them touching him, but the white wolves were too powerful for him to fight and he knew it. He sneered at Little White Crown. In his heart he hated him.

Shorty Bean saw just over the hill, a group of creatures walking towards the assembly. It was hard to see who they were so far off, but they came closer; it was quite the motley crew. Ms. Nora wearing metal armor; her broom was decked out in hammered metal. Tripod's shell shined with buffed bronze and Ben-Jeer the king Frog with his scales flecked in gold mesh, was holding a fish glass water tank and Sir Davy was inside thrashing around. The Beatles and other creatures from the kingdom of Ben-Jeer held Ms. Patty and the purple rose on a chair, carrying them from behind.

Shorty Bean's locket radiated a bright light and opened by itself. A great wind came from the locket, and a seal was placed on all the creatures which were on the right side of Little White Crown. The seals resembled a brilliant light. When all those who stood for good were sealed, the locket closed and the evil scattered back into the woods. "It has begun," said Little White Crown with authority.

General Polio motioned to the otter brigade, and following his signal they dispersed as troops, some on foot and some underground. They scattered like roaches. The general's heart remained hardened. He wanted what the light had to offer, but he was unwilling to change his ways to walk in it. Many struggle with that. They would rather have their own way, and in the end, it leaves them feeling betrayed and bitter.

Chapter Fourteen

The Gathering

L ittle White Crown needed to go alone in the forest and meet with his Father. He often retreated into quiet places to talk to him. His Father gave him wisdom, guidance and strength. "Hold tightly to your locket," he said to Shorty, and then he walked in the thicket of the woods. The trees bent over to protect any other animals or people from following him.

Sir Davy thrashed in the glass fish tank and Smarty was intrigued. He pressed his lips against the glass just to aggravate Sir Davy. Sir Davy retorted by smacking his tail against the glass. Norm used his antennas to wire in deep ocean noises from underwater whales, this made him nuts. He placed his fins over his head to minimize the annoying noise.

The sounds were piercing, and he was used to it living in a lake, not an ocean. Once Shorty realized what the two of them were doing, she reprimanded them and apologized to Sir Davy for their unnecessary and most aggravating behavior.

Little White Crown appeared and motioned for Shorty Bean and Smarty to accompany him into the deep forest. They followed him to Thunder Rail Lake. At the water's edge the waves raged, and there was no way any of them could cross. If only Tripod was with them.

Suddenly, there was a large explosion in the sky, and like a bullet Tripod landed right behind Little White Crown, smoke and all. Tripod bowed his head, rotated his mechanical leg, "At your service, great one!" he said as his shell flung open! He reached inside and pulled out a remote-control panel which had seven florescent square buttons. Two of them were yellow, two of them were blue, two of them were green and one larger than all the others was the color of red.

When he pressed the florescent green button, a secret numeric code appeared above it. It was a series of numbers. He pressed the code into the keyboard panel turning his back from them so they could not see what he entered. He was able to see the parameter and rock structure under the water. He calculated the stones underneath to form a pathway to walk across the water. He pressed the red button, but nothing happened. "Maybe I calculated that wrong." He said, it appeared the formula was malfunctioning, stones were randomly popping up from the water, but also going back down just as fast! Then Little White Crown put his wing around Tripod, and everything began to click. This time he realized, only press one button at a time.

Then Shorty Bean heard an evil laugh. It was the beaver from the cottage. How did he get into the Gazman Forest? Shorty Bean saw tiny trees being shredded like woodchips. Piles and piles of them were there, and the beaver was running back and forth along the water's edge.

Shorty took Smarty and reached him up on her shoulders so he could see the crazy beaver. Smarty's red cape kept flying into her face, and she was trying to blow it up into the air away from her eyes. An otter wondered off into the woods. He was a smaller fellow with yellow eyes. His name was Chance. He befriended Little White

Crown, and they had private conversations. It seemed as though they were longtime friends.

The forest has ears, and someone is always watching. WOOT WOOT! A red barn owl screeched from branches of a tree as they passed by his nest. They continued to travel through the rocks along the river, and then they came to dry land.

Then suddenly, Little White Crown stopped and said, "Who's following me? Show yourself." Jade had turned from a tree cover to himself. He had been hiding within the forest, spying on them.

"It is I, Jade, little ruler of the forest," he jeered at him. Tripod rotated his mechanical leg, preparing to attack him, but Little White Crown intervened and said, "Stop at once. Let this evil wolverine go!"

"That was kind of you . . . little wise one. You are weak just like your Father," Jade jeered. Tripod burned with fury towards Jade. He adored Little White Crown and highly honored him, after all he was the son of White Cloud, the ruler of the forest.

Anger burned within him until finally his shell popped open as his muscles bulged just like the incredible hulk. His mechanical leg extended which made it look a little like a beefed-up boot. He turned toward Jade with an intensity that let him know he would protect Little White Crown at any cost.

A bright light shown. It radiated from the heart-shaped locket around Shorty's neck. Its light blinded Jade. The power of the locket was unleashed. He couldn't stand its light. "It's not over, Little one!" Jade instantaneously hid his face, screeching in agony. He ran back to the heavily wooded forest so he could hide from the light. Tripod came down from his furry and back to his original size. "Go back where you came from," his voice echoed through the trees.

There was stillness that echoed as a shadow appeared over the skies above them. White Cloud called to his son and he cried back to him several times. Shorty Bean and Smarty ran to Little White Crown and put their arms around him and held him tightly.

Little White Crown loved when they ran to him, because he was a source of great comfort. Shorty asked him, "Are you going to die?"

"Yes, I am, but my death is not what you think, I will rise again and go to where my Father is," he said. I want to go where you go," she said.

He chuckled at her innocence and love in her heart for him. "Yes, you can, and your faith will get you there. You keep believing in me and the plans I have for this forest and for you. No one can snatch you or take you away from me. I will always be with you . . . forever." The heart-shaped locket fell off her neck and landed gently on the moss which grew on the forest floor, a protective place to keep the locket from damage,

Just when he had finished saying all this, Jade the wolverine ran past them and sneered. Little White Crown looked at him sternly, and he dropped his head in shame. He wanted the locket; he craved its power. He lunged for the locket and reached his paw towards it; the light peered through the sides and burned his eyes.

Tripod's voice changed and he changed as if he was from New York, the Bronx. "Little White Crown, are you sure you don't want me to take care of this guy? Really, it's no bother at all."

He laughed; Tripod was tenacious! "You're lucky, Jade, I don't put the hurting on you. He's holding me back!" Tripod made sure that statement was loud so wherever Jade the wolverine was, he would hear his intimating voice.

Frantically, Jade ran through the forest to reach General Polio and the army of otters. They had set pitfalls everywhere, and he was cautious not to step on one. That could mean certain death. He came upon the army of otters and asked to speak to the General. The otters gathered around him with weapons drawn. They held him until he came out of the wooden stick tent.

"General Polio, otter in charge of the brigade, I have come with news," Jade said. "What news do you have for me?" he inquired.

"There is a traitor among you," Jade said. He began to show his yellow teeth in a low menacing growl.

"How do you know this?" General Polio inquired, raising his metal arm braces.

"I heard them in the woods, talking about your plans. An otter, his name is Chance. They are on their way to destroy what you have built." The otters talked among themselves.

General Polio immediately spoke, "Rally up the otters, gather all the weapons, sharpen the pinecones." Standing behind them all by himself was a white spotted tiger named MJ.

"MJ, go and get my thistle weeds and bundle them," he commanded. MJ lived in the caves just outside of the forest. He kept to himself because he struggled to breathe on his own, but when his family died, General Polio helped him with food and water and invented a mechanism which helped him catch his breath. For that he was indebted to him for service anytime he needed it.

"Grab the fire casings of walnuts and close the entrances to your wooden huts." MJ had an apparatus under his neck. He reached his paw and took a deep breath; he was asthmatic.

General Polio said, "That is all we need from you, Jade." Then the army of otters took their weapons and placed them at the wolverine. "But wait, let me join you. You and I are a lot alike!" Jade fell to the ground, "You wouldn't kill me now, would you?"

General Polio said, "We won't if you take us to this Little White Crown. We want to see him for ourselves." Then Jade the wolverine agreed, and they ran quickly with him through the Gazman Forest. Shorty Bean knew it was time to be getting back to the cottage. She told Little White Crown she would be back soon.

Chapter Fifteen

Where Have You Been?

Shorty Bean knew they had to go back to the cottage, so they followed the pathway, passing the purple rose to the backyard. There was Grandma Ellie and Mom sitting on the back deck. Grandma Ellie was petting Mrs. Patty, and she was soaking it up.

"Where have you been?" Grandma questioned

"We were just sitting in the rose garden . . . looking at the clouds in the sky. You would never believe what we saw." "Aw, to be young again, imagination, dreaming, adventure. When you get my age, it's hard to get around," Grandma Ellie mentioned. "Isn't that right, Mrs. Patty?" Mrs. Patty purred, wrapping her tail around her arm. As Dad stepped out onto the porch, he asked, "Why do you dress that raggedy old cat in clothes and nylons? It's just plain strange!" He never truly understood fashion.

"Oh, calm down. She likes it. It makes her happy. The nylons keep her legs warm in the winter. She is an outside cat, you know." "Oh yeah, that makes complete sense," he retorted, meanwhile thinking what a loon Grandma was. Mom chimed in, "That's enough!" She knew it was time for her husband to shut his mouth.

"You two go inside and get yourself cleaned up!" Grandma Ellie already placed sheets of old newspapers on the table." Mom said, "Awesome, we love decorating eggs."

Shorty washed her hands, and Smarty was forced to go back to the bathroom. His paws were fifthly. "Clean paws or no eggs!" Shorty commented. He huffed and

puffed all the way to the bathroom, where he pulled up a step stool and began to scrub. Smarty released the soap dispenser one too many times and was flooding the bathroom with bubbles. Shorty wondered where he could be. She left the kitchen to see what he was up to. When she made it to the bathroom, he had soap suds on his chin and cheeks. He looked like Santa Claus.

When hamdogs are silent, be alerted, very alerted! "Oh, Smarty!" she said as she wiped his face clean with a laundered towel. Smarty did not like when Shorty cleaned his face. She always rubbed too hard irritating his nose and making him sneeze. ACHOO! "Bless you!" she exclaimed.

Grandma Ellie had cooked around thirty eggs. There was yellow, orange, red, green, purple, blue and pink dye.

Smarty loved eggs. On occasion Grandma Ellie would make him a batch of scrambled eggs in his dish. She always said they were good for his fur coat. When Shorty was not looking, Smarty popped the top of three eggs, now damaged. They would be an afternoon snack. However, after they were finished decorating the Easter eggs, Shorty wanted to take the broken ones outside and feed them to the animals. Smarty was beside himself. He had a plan, a pretty good one as far as he was concerned. It worked every year, but this one! "Aw, Phooey!" Smarty grumbled under his breath!

As they left the cottage, a trail of colored paw prints were imprinted on the kitchen floor. Once outside, Shorty Bean thought she would hide a few further out back. That way the animals would not get used to being fed too close to the cottage.

As she started to hide the eggs, she felt a sick feeling coming over her, a pressure on her chest! "Smarty, I don't feel good." She collapsed, falling to the ground.

There stood an army of otters. They were heading towards the kingdom of Ben-Jeer. Jade the wolverine was leading the charge to Thunder Rail Lake. When they arrived at the waters edge, a fishing line with a sharpened hook was lowered into the water. The current was strong this time of year. Sir Davy noticed the hook and tried to avoid it, but the current was too much for him. He fought the best he could until his tail flipped into the hook and snagged him.

They jerked him out of the water. "Where is this Little White Crown?" the otters asked.

Sir Davy would not answer. Sir Davy said, "I am a soldier in your army, or a traitor." They pulled him onto the shore and bound his fins in chains. He gasped for breath as they mocked him and kicked him. One of the otters took pity on him, and when General Polio was not paying attention, he brought him a paw cup filled with lake water. Sir Davy was grateful for this act of kindness.

A fish cannot be out of the water for long periods of time, and if he did not get back in soon, he would perish. All the otters screamed at Sir Davy, "Traitor! Traitor!" Just then, Little White Crown flew down and swooped over Sir Davy and pulled him up into the sky.

Sir Davy took a deep breath, gasping for water. Little White Crown realized how serious this was. He needed to get him to safe waters so he could breathe again.

Then he slowly dropped him down in the water. Immediately he swam to the depths of the lake, regenerated and strengthened. White Cloud flew back and placed his claws on the ground and said, "You ask who Little White Crown is. I am he, the one you seek."

"Seize him!" General Polio shouted! "Seize him, seize him!" all the otters shouted in unison.

Little White Crown did not put up a fight. He surrendered willingly. They carried him to White Clouds nest, jeering him and mocking him on the way. When they arrived, they bound his wings so he could not fly. They made him walk up the tree stairs to the top of his nest. It was hard for him; the weight of his wings were heavy and he was weary and tired. He wanted to give up so many times, but when he felt like giving up, he heard the cry of his Father, White Cloud. It gave him the confidence to rise to the challenge and continue.

Then, when he reached the top of the nest, they set the winding tree branches on fire by catapulting walnut bombs. In no time at all the tree blazed with fire. The otters gathered around the base of the tree, shouting,

"Traitor! Traitor!" Chance hid away from them. Tears flooded his eyes; he loved Little White Crown and knew the evil that devised a plan to hurt him. "Why are you crying? Are you sad your weak ruler will die today?" From the shadows and smoke Jade appeared. "Why don't you go help him. Are you afraid you might burn your fur?" "Leave me alone!" he responded.

MJ jumped in front of him, and Jade tore the apparatus from his neck which helped him to breathe. MJ was in trouble. He struggled to breathe on his own. Little White Crown had no way down for the nest and he could not fly. All the otters watched from below. They were chanting, dancing and laughing. General Polio relished in their hate towards him, but MJ was humbled by his presence and bowed his head in reverence.

Chapter Sixteen

Pride Is Broken

The fire ignited even more, then suddenly they heard the nest crack in half and Little White Crown fell through the split tumbling down into the fiery coals beneath. When he reached the bottom of the tree, sparks flew all around him. But even amid the fiery mess, he was unharmed. Not one feather on his head or chest was burned.

At first, this troubled the otters. After all, he should have been scorched. Little White Crown turned his head, closed his eyes, and he gasped for breath as General Polio intently watched him. With a look of kindness and piercing eyes, he said, "May your pride be broken!" The forest darkened and became eerily quiet.

MJ slowly walked behind General Polio gasping for breath, "Why . . . won't . . . you . . . relent?" Then he fell to the ground out of utter exhaustion, barely breathing, for the smoke had compromised his breathing.

The ground shook, the hills trembled and down came White Cloud, the ruler of the Gazman Forest. He set his retractable gold lens directly on General Polio! The braces on his arms broke off, and his weak legs strengthened, his muscles increased.

General Polio fell on his paws, "I'm sorry, please forgive me," but it was too late! He should have asked for forgiveness while Little White Crown was alive. General Polio had compassion on MJ and tried to revive him. The black bears roared, and the black ravens cried. Darkness had won. Was all hope lost? A dark cloud loomed over the forest for three days. The General lay prostrate on the ground, weeping at a still MJ with no sign of life. He would not eat or drink anything!

White Cloud placed a hedge of protection around his son. No animal or beast was able to touch his body. The animals who loved him grieved.

On the third day, something happened. Rainbows exploded throughout the sky. The color of the sky itself was brilliant blue. Although the sun shone, thunder billowed from the clouds and lightning flashed. The animals of the forest were confused. No one could understand what was going on.

Then instantly, Little White Crown opened his eyes, and his feathers began to fluff. White Cloud swooped down from the sky on beams of the sun, and his light reflected in his eyes. The tree vines which bound him broke off, and White Cloud helped him to his feet!

"Are you ready?" he asked as he pulled out his wooden skateboard from behind his massive wing. "Ready, Father," he replied. Little White Crown skated around the tree. With each swirl, the tree began to come to life again. The nest was being rebuilt right before the forest's eyes.

Shorty Bean woke up from sleeping, "He's alive!" she yelled, "Who is alive?" Smarty asked.

"Little White Crown. They killed him, but he is alive. We have to go see him."

Smarty was concerned about Shorty Bean; she didn't look right. Her face was pale and her cheeks rosy in color, "Let's go back to the cottage," Smarty said, Shorty agreed!

So, they headed back to the cottage; and as soon as Shorty came in, her mom looked at her and asked, "What is wrong?"

Shorty Bean replied, "I am really tired all of a sudden and need to go and lie down and get some rest."

Mom thought that she might have a fever. She felt the top of her forehead. She did not feel warm at all, but rather cool to the touch. "No fever, just go upstairs and lay down," she told her.

As Shorty lay down in bed, she couldn't help but think of the vision she saw, it was so real. How could anyone want Little White Crown dead? It seemed rather odd. However, she was glad that he was alive again.

Smarty left the bedroom for a snack. He was craving a crisp apple. Shorty held her locket as tears gently rolled down her face. Smarty jumped on the kitchen counter and grabbed a nice red and green apple from the basket. He took a quick bite. It was delicious, so he finished it off; and his cheeks were stuffed with apple bites. He looked like a hamster.

"Where is my snack?" she asked him, "Monoester, norp shure," he mumbled. Norm the tick had been quiet for a while. It must have been a bad connection. He echoed back to her. "Where have you been?" Smarty asked. Norm did look confused; after all, he couldn't understand Smarty's gibberish.

He replied, "Where have you been?" He was back to his old self. "I miss White Cloud!" she said.

"Hold the locket and believe. You must ask for White Cloud to come and see us!" he said.

Shorty closed her eyes and heard stomping on the rooftop. At this hour, who could it be?

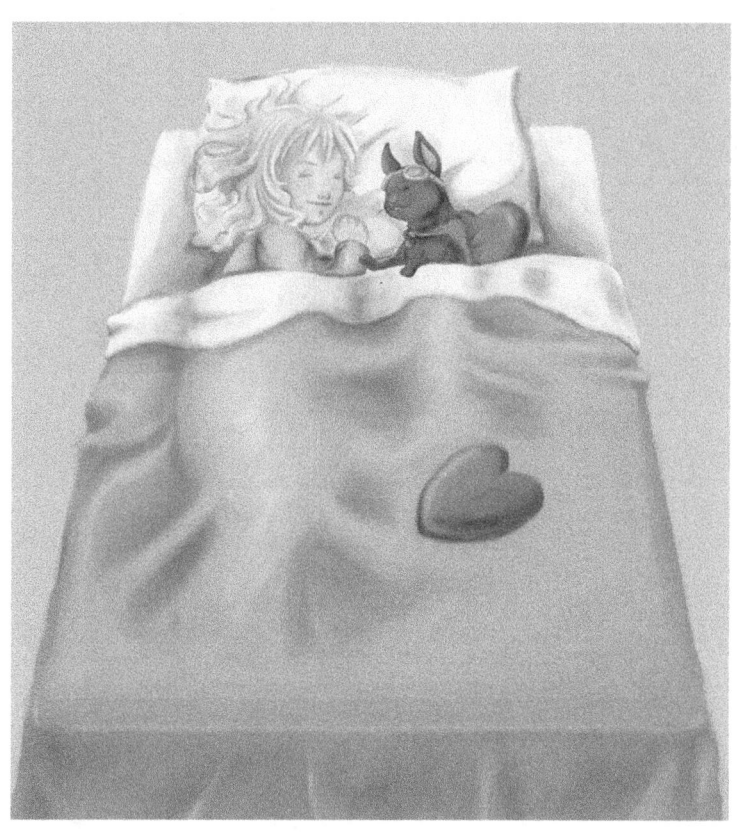

Chapter Seventeen

Trained Aviators

S horty Bean went to the window. There she discovered it was Tripod. He was walking strategically around the rooftop picking up walnuts. He motioned for her to stay put! After all, walnuts in the Gazman Forest are like hand grenades, and he had his share of experiences before.

"What are you doing here?" she asked. "I am checking to see if you are all right," he replied. "That is very sweet and thoughtful of you, Tripod. I am feeling much better." "Good to hear!" he remarked.

White Cloud was at the front of the house, and he whispered to Tripod, "SHUSH, don't say a word!" Tripod winked. Shorty Bean noticed the shadow of his wings. She was excited. "White Cloud!" She ran onto the rooftop and gave him the biggest hug. Another bird came soaring down. Guess who it was? Little White Crown. Shorty Bean asked if he would take her and Smarty flying just like White Cloud did.

The golden heart-shaped locket Shorty Bean found was powerful, and its power is not just contained inside the locket. The locket is only a symbol of its true power. Many seek the power for their own personal gain, and many desires come from a corrupt heart. People often fear what they cannot control, and the power of the very Spirit cannot be controlled. There are many intricate parts of the power, and each one serves a greater purpose. One must have an unshakable faith—faith just like a child to have the mystery revealed to them

We cannot control the wind, but with training and a little faith we can learn to navigate through it.

"Father, what do you think about us flying together?" he asked.

White Cloud replied, "Sure!"

Shorty Bean climbed on Little White Crown's back. She was nervous, but she trusted him because of his Father! She was safe, right?

Little White Crown jokingly said, "I would hang on tightly if I were you. I have not been flying as long as my Father. GET READY!" With a loud cry they were off!

White Cloud chuckled, "Don't worry if he drops you, I will catch you!" He zoomed his retractable gold lens toward his son, Shorty and Smarty. Targets were in full sight. White Cloud flew beneath them just to make sure everything was kosher.

They flew in and out of the clouds like trained aviators. Once they reached the right altitude, they joined wings and White Cloud spun his son around to the point he became dizzy. Smarty looked as though he was going to upchuck, probably because he ate way too much fruit just a few hours beforehand.

Meanwhile, back at the cottage, Dad and Mom had hired a local pilot to fly them around town. Grandpa Andy and Grandma Ellie did not like airplanes very much, so they declined to go, plus Shorty was sleeping, so they didn't want to disturb her.

The city airport was basically a landing strip with an office, gas station and a hangar to house small planes— not a big place at all! So, Mom and Dad hopped aboard the airplane and clicked their seatbelts into place, safety first. The pilot radioed in his location, started the engine and checked his controls. Everything was clear, so up, up and away they went. Mom was excited. She had never seen the cottage at this vantage point before, it was a whole new world.

As she was looking out the window, she saw something, it looked like a red cape. Norm engaged his antennas, potentially to reach any other brown-legged ticks from space; after all, that is where ticks come from, so they say!

"Heavenly noodles, that looks like Smarty." Just then, the pilot mentioned that his controls were malfunctioning. They began to swerve in and out of the clouds. Mom's stomach was getting squeezy, but Dad was a thrillist. He was having the time of his life!

Smarty happened to glance over and noticed it was Mom staring at him from the plane window; he quickly placed his red cape over his head in hopes that he would remain undetected.

Dad said, "Yeah, right, that would be the day when Hamdog's fly."

White Cloud and Little White Crown brought Smarty and Shorty back to the cottage. The time for visiting her grandparents was coming to an end.

"I am going to miss you both!" she said. Shorty Bean wondered about what was to come. The battle had started, but never went anywhere. White Cloud reassured her that in due time she would understand. Although Shorty Bean wanted to know what would happen in the future, sometimes you just have to wait it out and see for yourself!

"We are always with you, Shorty Bean. Whenever you need us, just hold the locket and believe." Smarty's cape was filled with adventure remembrances, but still had room for a few more. Grandma Ellie wasted no time sewing them on!

"All done," Grandma Ellie said as she placed the red cape back on Smarty's neck. It was a tad bit heavier, but he wore it well. So many memories were on his red cape. There were pictures of Ms. Nora, Tripod, Sir Davy, Ben-Jeer and Little White Crown, Mrs. Patty, the purple rose, the white wolves and so many other creatures just to name a few.

Shorty Bean reflected, pondering her adventures and the time she had in the Gazman Forest. She admired her seashell diamond ring and remembering how she got it in the depths of the ocean with White Cloud. Truly precious times...

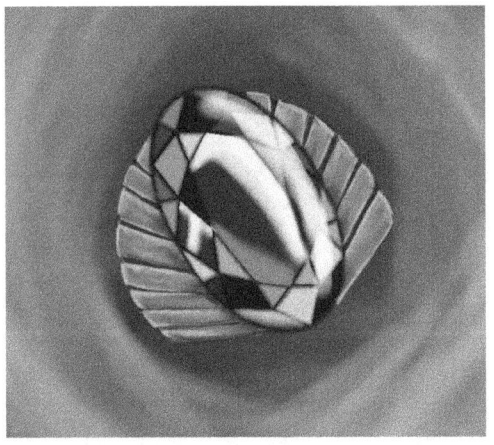

The warrior had finally come. Little White Crown, the son of White Cloud, a gift to everyone. As Ms. Nora said, "He came to save us from doom and gloom." Indeed, he did, but what about the battle? When would it begin?

No one really knew of the day or the hour, only White Cloud, the ruler of the Gazman Forest.

Shorty wanted to know as curiosity burned inside of her. Of course, she wanted to know everything, don't we all? but sometimes we cannot know everything; that is not always a bad thing, but rather a good thing!

Dad packed the truck, and they spent time giving each other hugs before they left. Shorty Bean held onto them; she did not want to go. Smarty jumped in the backseat waging his tail Dad yelled at him, and said, "On the floor, Smarty." He looked at him and took down his eyeglasses.

Everyone said their good-byes. Grandpa Andy gave Shorty Bean a big hug. Grandma Ellie told her that she loved her.

White Cloud had told Shorty Bean that there would be a battle of good and evil. When would this battle begin? No one knew, but only White Cloud. One thing was for sure, Little White Crown would return to the forest. And for now, Shorty Bean was determined to hold on to the locket and the power within.

On the ride back to the cities, Mom turned up the radio and Dad leaned over to give her a kiss on the cheek. Shorty Bean and Smarty snuggled in the backseat.

Shorty Bean wiggled her toes admiring her beloved daisy toe ring. She could not wait to visit her grandparents' cottage again soon. For now, she would dream of her adventures and wait for the battle to begin.

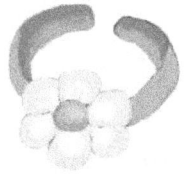

About the Author

Holly Szurpicki was born in Detroit, Michigan, the car capital of the world. Although she couldn't drive yet, her imagination had a way of taking her wherever she dreamed to go.

Holly wished one day to be a princess, a park ranger or an entrepreneur. She states, "Two out of three is not too shabby."

She is passionate about creating stories, screenplays and writing songs. Holly began writing a manuscript in the year 2001, which lay dormant as she focused on raising her two children. But when the year 2008 arrived, she teamed up with a virtual animation studio out of New York. That is when the dream came to life, and the Shorty Bean story became her first novel.

Art and individual creativity have tremendously inspired her throughout her career. Holly possesses visual creativity which takes her to places beyond words to live animation in her mind. Being able to envision her characters and their environments is a true gift, and she recognizes this as supernatural.

Despite many tragic circumstances she has faced throughout her life, Holly has always maintained a positive attitude and loves to encourage others to pursue their God-given dreams.

Her goal for writing children's books is to create a safe and wholesome environment for imagination. Holly desires for children to DREAM BIG, and never forget that there is nothing impossible with God. She believes each one of us has a divine destiny and wants others to never be afraid to pursue their dreams.

Holly lives in northern Minnesota with her husband and two children and a water dog named Klause. She loves the outdoors, photography and fishing, to name a few of her passions.

For more information regarding
the Shorty Bean series, future works
or general inquiries,
check out her website:
www.hollykszurpicki.com